MERGER

Chelle
Bliss
xoxo

MERGER

COPYRIGHT © 2017 BY CHELLE BLISS

All rights reserved. No part of this book may be reproduced or transmitted in any form, including electronic or mechanical, without written permission from the publisher, except in the case of brief quotations embodied in critical articles or reviews.

This is a work of fiction. Names, characters, businesses, places, events, and incidents are either the products of the author's imagination or used in a fictitious manner. Any resemblance to actual persons, living or dead, or actual events is purely coincidental. This book is licensed for your personal enjoyment only.

This book may not be resold or given away to other people. If you would like to share this book with another person, please purchase an additional copy for each person you share it with. If you are reading this book and did not purchase it, or it was not purchased for your use only, then you should return it to the seller and purchase your own copy. Thank you for respecting the author's work

Cover Art by Okay Creations
Edited by Lisa A. Hollett
Proofread by Julie Deaton, Rosa Sharon, & Fiona Wilson
Interior Design by Chelle Bliss

www.chellebliss.com

ISBN-13: 978-1682306154
ISBN-10: 1682306151

First Edition

Dedication

To my grandparents,
Thank you for your unwavering love and support. I love you more
than words can ever express. I'd be nothing without you.
Love always, Chelle

*"Invincibility lies in the defense;
the possibility of victory in the attack"*

— Sun Tzu

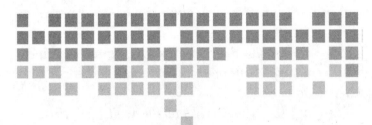

Chapter 1

Antonio

Settling between Lauren's legs, I twist my hips and grind my cock against her softness. "I'm not ready to say goodbye."

Her fingers tangle in my hair as she wraps her arms around my neck. "We still have a few hours." She gazes up at me with a sinful smile.

The sun streams through the windows, illuminating the bed and bathing us in warmth. The distant claps of thunder mingle with the waves crashing near the shore as if serenading us to stay. I'm not ready to face reality or the people we are once we step foot off the island.

The hardness I'd seen in Lauren inside the walls of Interstellar has vanished in the last two days, replaced by the beautiful, delicate creature underneath me. "Let's stay another day." Burying my face in her neck,

I breathe in the saltiness of her skin before pressing my lips against her.

She turns her head, giving me free rein to feast on her flesh, but she doesn't speak.

I slide my hand down her side before gripping her hip in my palm and repeating the words. "Let's stay another day."

"We can't," she whispers, peering up at me, and I know she's right although I don't want to hear it. "We have to go back."

Leaving the island will put the wall back between that has been eroding. Slowly, brick by brick, the real Lauren has emerged, showing me parts of her I never knew existed. The woman underneath is tough as I expected, but her dreams aren't her own. She's driven by the memories of her father, and she's burying herself in her work instead of living life.

My lips skim her neck before finding her mouth. "Promise me things won't go back to the way they were," I say, staring into her eyes, searching for affirmation that the entire weekend wasn't just a ruse.

"Antonio, I..."

I crush my mouth to hers, sealing whatever she was going to say inside. They're words I'm not ready to hear because I know the wall will return as soon as we step foot off the beach. The only thing I can do is remind her of what it's like to be one. How truly compatible we are and how together we can make magic happen.

She moans as my fingers slide underneath her ass, tipping her hips upward for better access. Every moment she's been in my presence I've had to fight the urge to bury myself inside her because it is the only time I feel at peace and truly fulfilled.

When I push my cock inside, she wraps her legs around me, holding me close. I open my eyes, gazing down at her as our bodies are one. I wish I could freeze time. This moment is pure perfection, but just like everything, it's fleeting and impossible to capture for eternity.

I slide in and out of her, relishing the feel of her body tightening around mine with each sweep. There's no denying what's between us. No matter what she says when we land in Chicago, I feel the way her body craves me. I know in my bones that she's just as in love with me as I am with her.

"Find out everything you can about Trent Moore," I bark into the phone.

Less than an hour ago, I arrived at Interstellar to get Lauren's decision on the merger between our companies. It was the only way I could think to keep our relationship alive and salvage the mess that's become of the Cozza-Interstellar takeover. I'd given Lauren the day to think it over and share it with her team before she'd give me the final answer to bring back to Cozza.

But Lauren was nowhere to be found. Cassie hadn't seen her for at least 3 hours, and there's nothing written in her datebook that gives any of us a clue as to where she may be. I scoured her office, searching for some shred of evidence, but I found nothing.

Slowly, panic crept in, and my worst fears were realized. Lauren isn't the type to disappear without a word, especially not when the future of Interstellar is on the line.

Panicked, I did the only thing I could. I called the head of security at Cozza and made finding Lauren a top priority. I didn't want to involve her team because that would set off alarm bells throughout the company and cause widespread panic, and it wasn't something either of us could afford. Maverick, my head of security, is usually busy keeping our company secrets safe or tossing trespassers from our testing facility just outside the Chicago city limits, but nothing is more important than finding Lauren.

"Give me an hour," he tells me.

"You have thirty minutes." I hang up before Maverick can reply.

I'm done wasting another second discussing the details when he should be searching for her and Trent. With each passing minute, she's moving farther away and becomes harder to find. In the possible few hours she's been missing, she could be hundreds of miles away and even harder to trace.

I slam my cell phone down on Lauren's desk, filled with so much rage I could easily crush it in my palm. "Goddamn it." The screen splinters into a hundred pieces under my palm from the impact.

The only thing that matters now is finding her, and I won't rest until she's found alive.

But Trent is smart. Finding him won't be as easy. With his head start and ability to hide his digital footprint, my team is going to have to be creative and hope he fucks up somehow.

But there's one thing I know. I will find him. I will not stop until he pays for what he's done and I have Lauren back in my arms. If Trent harms one hair on her head, his punishment will be a hundred times more painful than what he did to her.

My phone rings, a shard of glass pricking my finger as I answer. "Yeah?"

"You better come over here," Cassie says.

I did not want her to go there alone, but Cassie insisted on going to Lauren's apartment in hopes of finding her there. I knew the likelihood Cassie would find her was almost zero, but I wasn't going to stop her.

"She there?"

"No, but..." Her voice trails off, and she whimpers.

"Cassie?" I stalk toward the elevator, ready to kill Trent and anyone else who is involved in Lauren's disappearance.

"Someone destroyed her place. It's like something out of a movie, Mr. Forte."

I stab at the button inside the elevator, smearing my blood across the L. "Don't call the police. I'll be there in ten minutes."

"Yes, sir."

The last thing I need, or Lauren needs, for that matter, is to have her disappearance become media fodder. It would be a nightmare both personally and for our companies. If the police were to investigate her whereabouts leading up to her kidnapping and find out about our trip to my private island, the media will have a field day with the knowledge that the CEOs of both Cozza and Interstellar are romantically involved.

As I walk toward Lauren's building, I call Maverick back and ask him to meet me at her penthouse to gather any evidence that may lead to her rescue.

Cassie's waiting in the lobby for me with her head down, pacing, and mumbling gibberish to herself.

"Cassie?"

She stops moving, lifts her head, and our eyes lock.

The panic I felt multiplies. Visions of Lauren injured or worse flash through my mind, and I'm momentarily frozen by fear before I collect myself, rushing to Cassie's side.

"It's not good." She shakes her head and starts to pull at the ends of her hair. "God, it's awful."

I reach out to her, touching her arms. "Stay down here."

She goes rigid and peers up at me with narrowed eyes. "I can't stand here and do nothing, Mr. Forte. I can't."

"Take me up, then. We'll figure it out together."

She moves toward the bank of elevators on the other side of the lobby, staring at the tiles on the floor as we walk. "Trent is a bastard, Mr. Forte, but I never thought he'd do this."

"We'll find her, Cassie. That I promise you." I stand beside her as the elevator doors close. We both stare at the floor, silent in our fear as the carriage rises toward Lauren's floor.

I know we'll find her, but heads are going to roll if... I can't let myself think that way. I can't give in to the possibility that we're not going to find her. The first forty-eight hours are the most critical in any investigation, and I plan to use all my resources, both legal and illegal, to track Trent down and rescue my girl.

Cassie glances up at me before the elevator doors open. "If anyone can find her, sir, I know you can."

In any other situation, her confidence in me would've made me smile, but I give her a quick nod instead because, for the first time in my life, nothing is certain.

I'm rocked back when the elevator doors slide apart, and I see the front door is open right into Lauren's penthouse loft. The beautiful hardwood floor is covered with her personal belongings, and shreds of her furniture are scattered everywhere. There isn't a spot left untouched, and not a single item is in its original form.

Stepping inside, I'm careful not to disturb much. "Did you see blood anywhere?"

Cassie shakes her head.

"Have you been here before?"

She nods.

"Anything missing from what you can tell?"

"No, sir." She stares out the windows across the living room, almost in a trance. "But it's such a mess in here I don't know if I could even tell if there was anything missing."

Cassie almost jumps two feet off the floor when Maverick pounds on the door. She's even paler than when I first arrived, and guilt floods me that she had to witness the mayhem in Lauren's apartment alone. If I had been thinking clearly, I would've had my security come here instead of Cassie.

"Don't be frightened, Cassie. I called my security team."

CHELLE BLISS

Maverick's not even two feet inside the penthouse when I start to question him. "Have you found out anything yet?"

"The team is working on it. I need a few minutes to survey the apartment for evidence, and then we'll talk." His eyes land on Cassie standing near the corner of the living room, staring down at the city. "She a witness?"

"She works for Ms. Bradley. She didn't see anything, but she knows Trent and Lauren's history and may be vital in helping to find out where he's taken her."

"We're one hundred percent sure he has her?"

"Yes," I bite out; my anger growing with every passing second that's being wasted.

Maverick answers his phone on the first ring. "Yeah? Tell me what you got." His eyes lock with mine, and he motions toward the hallway with his head before wandering away..

"Cassie," I say softly, approaching her with caution so I don't scare her any more than she already is. The poor woman is definitely on edge. She could've walked in on Trent or someone else and ended up dead. "I need to know everything about Trent and Lauren."

Cassie looks at me, but it's as if she is looking right through me, unable to focus. "Whatever you need," she says, almost in a whisper.

"Sir."

Maverick's deep voice startles Cassie again, pulling her from the trance. Reaching out, I steady her in my grip.

Maverick could scare the shit out of the calmest person. He's almost seven feet tall, with broad shoulders,

8

dark eyes, and looks more Neanderthal than most people on the streets. He's been a loyal employee for ten years, and I was lucky enough to snag him right after he retired from the Green Berets. With his connections all over the world, information is easy to access, and he's the most loyal person in my company.

I give Maverick an icy stare because he should know better than to creep around the penthouse quiet as a mouse and then speak. "Give me a few minutes with Cassie. Look around and see if you can find anything first."

"Will do." Maverick disappears quickly.

"Cassie, come sit." I push aside a pillow that's lying on the floor with the filling scattered about and make a place for us to sit.

She moves slowly and folds her hands in her lap as she sits, but she doesn't bring her eyes to mine. She's still staring out the window. If she's focusing on nothing or everything, I can't tell. Cassie has always been a talker, and rarely have I been in her presence that she isn't rattling off words so fast I can't keep up. But today, after everything that's happened, she's a ghost of her former self.

"What can you tell me about Trent and Lauren? I know it's an awkward conversation to have with me, but even the smallest bit of information may help us find them quicker."

Her fingers pick at the hem of her skirt, and her eyes follow their movement. She doesn't speak at first, and I don't push her.

"They started the Mercury project together, and after spending countless hours working together, things just happened." She peers up at me. "Lauren broke it off after she became CEO, but Trent..." she sighs and shakes her head. "Trent never could accept that they were over."

"Tell me more."

Cassie spends the next ten minutes telling me everything she knows about Trent and how he has treated Lauren over the last few years. It is hard for me to understand how Lauren kept him on as an employee with everything he'd done to her. But like many people in her situation, in our situation, we keep people whom we loathe for the good of the company.

The one thing I know for sure about Lauren is that Interstellar is the most important thing in her life. She'd sacrifice her comfort if it meant success for her employees and achieving her father's dream.

When Cassie's done, I leave her on the couch and find Maverick in Lauren's bedroom, picking through a pile of ripped up papers and photographs. "This one's interesting." He hands me a crumpled picture. Trent and Lauren are sitting side by side on a rock with a small cabin in the background. "If I kidnapped someone, this is exactly where I'd take them."

I grab the photo from his hand and study the image. A younger Lauren with a big, carefree smile on her face. Turning the photo over, the year 2012 is written on the back with the word Canada. "What did your contact have to say earlier?"

"They're piecing together his assets and background. He's done a good job covering his tracks. Based on the lack of information, I'd say he was planning this for a while. Dealing with foreign governments can be tricky too. But have no doubt, Mr. Forte, I'll find her."

"Fuck," I growl. "I don't care who we have to pay off, make it happen, Maverick."

"What do you want to do about the apartment?"

I look around, taking in the damage Trent caused. I would hate for Lauren to come back to such a mess, especially after everything she'll have been through.

"Get it cleaned up and replace everything that's damaged."

"It'll be done today."

"I'm going to take Cassie home. Call me as soon as you get more information."

"Yes, sir." Maverick reaches for his phone and heads for the elevator with me on his heels. "Leave everything to me." He glances at Cassie, who hasn't moved since I left her on the couch. "Ma'am." He smiles in her direction.

Her eyes wander up his body, but she doesn't return the smile. "Sir."

I motion for Cassie after the elevator doors close with Maverick inside. "Let's go. My team will handle the apartment."

She stands and stalks in my direction, crunching the broken pieces of debris on the floor with every step. "We should call the police."

"Not now."

She pokes my chest, and her eyes narrow as she stares up at me. "No. Now, Mr. Forte. The police will find her." She pokes me again, but a little harder. "You may have spent some time with Lauren, but how do I know you have her best interest at heart?"

"Cassie." I back away from her slender finger and daggerlike nail. "Come on. Don't be crazy."

Her eyes widen, and redness creeps up her neck as she steps forward and pokes me harder. "Crazy? You're the man trying to steal her company. I find it hard to believe that you have her best interest at heart."

I can't blame her. From the outside, I appear to be the enemy. No one really knows what happened on the island or the way Lauren has completely captivated me. She's like a drug that I crave and can't get out of my system. One taste and I was hooked.

No one has ever had that effect on me before. I've been with many women, more than I really care to admit, but I've never chased someone before her.

I wrap my hands around Cassie's arms, but I grip her gently. "Listen. If we call the police, the media will find out. It would be disastrous for Lauren and Interstellar if word about her abduction got out. No matter what you think, I'm doing what's best for Lauren."

She tenses and bares her teeth. "You better find her fast, or you won't be able to control what happens inside Interstellar."

Truer words have never been spoken. We only have a few hours to come up with a way to buy some time to keep the brass at Interstellar content with her absence.

"I'll handle it."

She pulls away and takes a deep breath as she tugs down her dress shirt that's come untucked from her knee-length skirt. "I'm sorry, Mr. Forte. I didn't mean to sound like a bitch, but I love Lauren like a sister. I like control, and I have none right now. I don't know what to say to anyone tomorrow morning."

"Let me take you home, and by the time you walk through the doors of Interstellar tomorrow, I'll either have Lauren back or I'll have a cover story for you to use to keep people from asking too many questions."

"You better make it good, Mr. Forte. Lauren never misses work, so it'll be a hard sell."

"Believe me, Cassie. I'll make it bulletproof."

She twists her lips, staring me in the eyes like she's reading my thoughts. With an assistant like Cassie, it's not hard to understand how Lauren has begun to conquer the world.

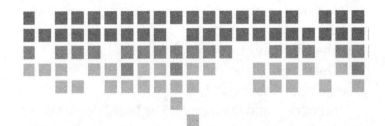

Chapter 2

Antonio

"We have to move on this," Carlino, my second-in-command at Cozza, says before I even have a chance to step two feet into our Chicago office.

I didn't sleep at all last night. I couldn't get Lauren off my mind. Was she okay? Was Trent treating her right? Was she still alive? Was she was thinking of me? It's a selfish thought to have, but I couldn't help myself. She had to know I'd move heaven and earth to find her.

No matter what's happening between our companies, our relationship is entirely separate and means more to me than anything else. Her safety is my top priority and the only thing that weighs on my mind. I could not care less about the takeover or the merger. When I told her there are more important things in life than work, I meant it.

Maverick and I spoke on the phone no less than ten times after I dropped Cassie off at her apartment. He still had trouble finding information on Trent, but he had tracked down a few clues. So far, there hadn't been a single ping off any cellular towers from his phone number or a charge on any of his credit cards. The bastard was too smart for a rookie mistake like that. He knew he'd be easily traceable with technology.

I stalk toward the elevator with Carlino following close behind. "Move on what?"

"Interstellar and the merger. The board doesn't want to wait. We'd like to push them harder and make the deal a reality sooner rather than later."

I narrow my eyes and stab at the elevator button before I glare at him. "Can I at least make it to my office before you start barking in my ear, Carlino?"

He's always wanted my job. Ever since the first day he walked in the door, he wanted to overthrow me, but he couldn't pull it off. I'd become too powerful for him to have a chance, but it didn't mean he didn't have the balls to try at every turn.

He cracks his neck, rolling his head around his shoulders. "There's whispers, Antonio." Crossing his arms in front of his chest, he arches an eyebrow and smirks.

The doors open and we step inside. I bite my tongue, waiting for the doors to close to give us privacy before I turn my full attention to the man at my side. "Whispers?"

He swipes his hand through his overly greasy hair with a cocky smile. "About Ms. Bradley."

"Carlino." I ball my hand into a tight fist, but I resist the urge to punch him square in the jaw. Although I'd love to watch him fall to the floor like the little bitch he is. "I'd watch your tongue and be very careful with your next words."

His smile hardens as his chin juts out. "Based on your response, the whispers are true. Either you move on it today, or I'll bring a motion before the board along with a no-confidence vote for you, Antonio."

"I'll set up a meeting with Josh Goldman, VP of Interstellar, and you two can hash out the details and get the ball rolling."

He folds his arms and cocks a shoulder. "Too busy to take part in the most important business merger of the century?"

I'm two seconds from popping his smug face, but I know it's what he wants, and I have to control my anger. He's pushing my buttons, and for the first time, getting a reaction out of me. "The paperwork is standard, Carlino. I didn't think you needed me to hold your hand, but I will if it's necessary."

"I can handle it all by myself, but don't forget where your loyalties lie, Antonio. Someone might take your lack of attention right now the wrong way."

"Do your job, and I'll do mine. Don't test me." The doors open, and I leave Carlino hovering near the back because his office is on another floor. He gives me a smug chin lift as the elevator doors close.

I've never been able to stand him, and I've made sure that even though I'm not here often, he's as far away from me as possible when I am. If I had to spend one more minute with him, I would've ended up knocking him out and given him plenty of ammunition to use against me.

Once everything is done and the merger has taken place, I need to reevaluate the corporate structure of the new company. Carlino tops my list.

"Good morning, Mr. Forte," Marny, my executive assistant for the last ten years, greets me with a cup of espresso and a smile. "Mr. Maverick is in your office waiting for you."

I give her a courteous smile and take the espresso before excusing myself, trying not to seem overeager. When I enter, he's sitting at my desk, pecking away at the keys on my computer as he talks on the phone, and he glances up at me.

Motioning for him to stay put, I take the seat across from him, placing the espresso on the edge of the desk along with my cell phone. I listen to his words very carefully.

"Canada." Maverick's eyes meet mine.

Alarm bells go off, and the picture of Lauren and Trent flashes through my mind. It's the perfect place for him to take Lauren. Close enough, yet so far and out of local police jurisdiction. But he forgot one thing: my reach is wider than that of any police department.

"When you have the address, send it to me." He pauses and punches a few keys on the keyboard. "We won't need backup. We're trying to keep this off the radar."

He says a few more things to the person on the other end of the phone before he hangs up. Leaning back in the chair, he lets out a loud, relieved sigh. "We're almost certain Moore's in Canada. Our best guess is that he's taken her to that cabin in the photo."

"Are you guessing?"

"His license plate was spotted through some tolls heading in that direction. Our guess is that he's taking her across the border. But I'll find him, Mr. Forte. If I have my way, Ms. Bradley will be back on US soil before the sun sets."

"I'm coming with you."

There's no way in hell I'd let him go after her alone. I'm completely certain of his competency, but I want my face to be the first Lauren sees after her rescue. Not because I want to steal the spotlight, but because I want her to know that I care enough to put everything else on hold to find her.

Maverick studies me for a moment. "Antonio, it's not safe."

I reach for my espresso, needing the caffeine to get my ass in gear and my head on straight after such a long night. "There's nothing to discuss. I'll be by your side whether Lauren is at that cabin or not. I won't be able to rest until you find her. Understood?" I raise an eyebrow and stare at him over the top of my cup.

"Yes, sir. Whatever will make you happy, although I strongly advise against it."

"Just find her, and I promise not to put myself in harm's way if it can be avoided."

He gives me a quick nod. "I'll have the address before noon. My buddy in the Canadian Special Operations Forces is working on the location."

"Thanks, Maverick. Now give me a little while to get some business done and my day set so I can go with you."

"Sorry about using your computer," he says, rising from my desk and knocking his knuckles against the mahogany desk.

"Don't ever apologize for helping me. I don't know what I'd do without you."

He leaves without another word, and I know I have limited time to get the deal with Interstellar rolling before we slip off to Canada without being noticed.

"Josh Goldman, please." I click through the endless emails that have rolled in since last night as I wait for Josh to answer the phone. I have as much love for the man as I do Carlino.

"Goldman," Josh says as soon as he answers the phone.

"It's Forte. I'd like to set up a meeting today for you and my VP to discuss the merger."

"I don't think that's wise without Lauren here."

I roll my eyes. "Do you want the merger or not?"

"Lauren and I already discussed the merger, and we decided to present it to the board."

"Then there's no time to waste. Meet with Carlino today, and call an emergency board meeting as soon as possible. It's up to you two to convince the people behind Interstellar it's in their best interests that we merge. I'm sure you can make it happen, no?"

"I can make it happen, Mr. Forte. Lauren may be in command, but I have just as much sway as she does."

The number twos are always willing to step up and show off their ability. But no matter what they do, the people within the company know that they're back-climbers and are only looking out for themselves.

"Then make it happen. Carlino will be there at one to make sure you have all the details before you present it and get the deal closed."

"You won't be coming?"

I'm not sure if I hear disappointment or disdain in his voice. "I figure you and Carlino can handle it on your own. I have other important business to attend to."

"Seems to be a common theme lately," he says in a snarky tone, referring to Lauren's absence.

It seems that Cassie has been able to sell the lie to the staff at Interstellar and bought us a little time until Lauren's found. The media hasn't been alerted, and no one is in a panic. Let them gossip all they want about a supposed love affair between us; I'd rather that happen instead of the news of her disappearance splashed across the front page. Nothing sends a company into a nose dive quicker than a kidnapped CEO.

Lauren

I freeze, squeezing my eyes shut, and I swallow down the bile that's rising in my throat as the latch opens, scraping against the metal as the bolt moves.

Maybe he'll leave me alone, safe in the darkness, if he thinks I'm still unconscious. Being in this room scares me, but the thought of what Trent's capable of is far more frightening because of the unknown.

I knew he had an unhealthy obsession with me and that he never fully accepted or got over our breakup, but I never thought he'd do something like this. Until recently, he wasn't ever aggressive and he'd never pushed himself on me. But all the warning signs were there, slowly building to his breaking point. I should've seen it coming and put more distance between us. I should've fired him a long time ago, but I just couldn't. Letting the company and the invention come before anything else, I opened myself up to his attack, and it led to my being in this room.

There's a loud creak as the door opens, but I don't dare sneak a glance across the floor toward his feet. When his footsteps move closer and grow louder as he approaches, I hold my breath and wait for whatever comes next.

Will he keep me in this tiny room as a prisoner until someone finds me or until I die? Will he torture me or, dear God, rape me until he's had his fill? A day ago, I would've said Trent didn't have it in him, but after he choked me until I passed out, I know he's capable of anything.

Trent slides his hands under my back as he lifts me into his arms. My skin crawls as our bodies touch, and he holds me against his chest as he carries me. I stay limp, letting my arms flop as he takes heavy steps out of the room he's kept me locked inside. I want to run, push away and escape, but I'm seized by panic and too terrified to even breathe, let alone move.

"I know you're awake," he says as his fingers dig into my waist and hip. "You can stop the act, Lulu."

Fuck. I sag against him, defeated and knowing I have to face him. But I still have my strength and speed to outrun him. I just need to figure out where we are and get the hell out of here. I would do anything to break free and get away from the madman, even if it means dying for a chance at freedom.

I squint, blinded by the harsh lighting in the new room, and swallow down the sob that wants to break free. Do not cry. I've never been a crier, and I refuse to start now. I won't give him the satisfaction of knowing that he's terrorizing me or any inkling that I've given up hope because of him.

"Where are we?" I try to remain as calm as possible, knowing my life depends on my ability to keep my mind focused.

My insides are twisting because this man, someone I once thought I loved, has done this to me. This man choked me until I blacked out, but it takes a special kind of crazy to do that to someone they supposedly love.

I wipe everything away and think of only one thing... survival. If I play nice, maybe, just maybe, he'll let his guard down long enough for me to get away.

"Our favorite place."

My panic level ratchets up from scared to death to off the charts because I know exactly where he's taken me.

We're at his favorite place, a secluded cabin in Canada. The tiny house is set back miles from any main street, and the nearest neighbors are over a mile away. Too far for anyone to hear me scream if I were able to escape and near enough for him to track me down on foot if he's conscious when I make my move.

How long had I been out before I woke up in the blacked-out room? He had to drug me to keep me from waking up during the six-hour drive before crossing the border. I should've known that the dull throb in my head was caused by more than his hands wrapping around my neck.

"Why here?" My voice sounds distant, almost robotic. I'm in shock, but who wouldn't be in the same situation? I can't bring myself to look at him, the man who's now my captor.

He gently sets me down on the bed as if he might break me, which is almost comical. "Because I needed us to be alone."

I stare down at my partially clothed body, and my stomach rolls as bile rises again in my throat.

He reaches over me and grabs something near the top of the headboard, but I can't bring myself to look. When he reaches for my wrist, I pull away and try to curl into a ball. I want to cry and run, but I know there's no one and nothing for miles. "Leave me be," I say, fighting back the tears that are threatening to fall.

I can't cry. I won't cry. I can't give him that power to know how much he's affecting me.

"You either give me your wrist, or else I'll put you back in the darkness."

I don't know what's worse—the cold, hard darkness of the safe room or being out here with a deranged lunatic. I know that the second he puts me back in the room, there'll be no chance for escape.

The only way I'm getting out of here is if I play by his rules and let him chain me up. But giving myself over willingly isn't something I'm used to doing, especially when everything inside me is already screaming for me run.

I roll to my back and stare up at the rustic beams above the bed, still unable to look him in the face. I take a deep breath and close my eyes. "I would rather stay out here with you." The lie leaves an acidic taste in my mouth.

Trent doesn't speak as he lifts my arm toward the headboard. When he locks a cold, metal handcuff around my wrist, I refuse to make any noise.

"Don't worry, Lulu. It won't be like this forever. Soon we'll both be free."

Delusional doesn't even begin to describe Trent, and I fear I have to let myself spiral into his insanity before I can make it out of here alive.

I glance at him.

Big mistake.

Gone is the handsome, put-together man who wooed me years ago. He's been replaced by someone else with so much darkness in his eyes that it chills me to the bone. There's a wildness I haven't seen before. As if something in him has shifted into this savage creature before me.

The fear that had been simmering inside, barely kept at bay, starts to creep into every fiber of my body.

Chapter 3

Antonio

As the jet starts down the runway, Maverick unpacks a duffel bag full of weapons, placing them on the table between us. Less than an hour ago, Maverick's man in Canada called to verify that there has been activity at the cabin near Windsor, Canada. We're certain it's Lauren and Trent. Without hesitation, I readied the jet and left Carlino and Josh to hash out the future of our companies.

"We'll be on the ground in thirty minutes, sir," the pilot announces before the wheels lift off the ground.

If the merger deal falls apart, so be it. My heart isn't in it anymore. I have enough money in the bank to last me twenty lifetimes. I've achieved almost everything I wanted to in life, all but one...finding someone to call mine. Now that I've found her, I don't care about anything else other than bringing her back safely and shielding her from anything like this ever happening to her again.

Maverick sets a small black handgun in front of me, turning the grip in my direction. "Only use this if necessary, sir."

I stare him down, running my finger over the edge of the armrest. "I've fired a gun before. I think I'd surprise you with my accuracy."

A smile pulls at the corner of his lips. "I'm sure you're quite the Rambo, but the last thing I need is for you to kill the man. Dealing with the Canadian officials when there's a murder committed by a high-profile person would be a nightmare."

"Who says they'd find a body?"

Maverick pinches the bridge of his nose and shakes his head. "If the animal needs to be put down, please let me handle it, sir."

"If I have a better shot and Lauren's in grave danger, I won't hesitate to pull the trigger."

"Clusterfuck," he mutters. "Let's go over the terrain and area surrounding the cabin. I want to make sure we're on the same page before we go in there, guns blazing."

He pulls a folded piece of paper from his back pocket and smooths it out in from of us. He points at the small building in the center. "The cabin is located near the coast of Lake Erie with no inhabitants for at least one mile on each side."

I nod, studying the map as his finger slides across it. "Are we going in by sea or land?"

Maverick holds back a laugh. "By land, sir. We'll be taking this route through the forest from the side road." He taps the paper. "Then we'll take this path through the dense woods until the cabin comes into view."

"Then?" I lean forward, studying the image.

"Then we wait for night."

"Unacceptable." It's a little after two, and there are too many hours until darkness descends. I'm unwilling to leave Lauren in the hands of the madman for that long.

"Darkness will give us the greatest cover and our best chance to rescue Lauren without anyone getting harmed."

"We'll discuss timing after we land and have the cabin in view."

Maverick nods, knowing I'm not one for waiting, especially when something this important is on the line.

"We need to change," he says, lifting a second duffle bag onto the tabletop. "You can't go in there in your suit. We'll be spotted from a mile away."

I grab the clothes from his hands and quickly remove my business suit and slide on the camouflage pants and shirt. "It doesn't matter what I'm wearing as long as we get the job done."

He lifts a holster in my direction. "Do you know how this goes on?"

Without hesitation, I take the leather holster from his hands and fasten it around my body. "I have more experience than you'll ever know."

But I know Maverick knows everything about me. The man didn't agree to be number one in security at

Cozza without finding out every little thing about my life. He knows I'm an avid outdoorsman and love to hunt. I spent much of my twenties traveling the world and taking part in hunting expeditions in some of the most remote terrain on the planet. As I grew older and wiser, I no longer found hunting as thrilling, and my moral compass had shifted.

"I think we're ready." He grabs his outfit, excusing himself to the bedroom in the back of the plane.

I take the few moments alone to stare down across the landscape as Lake Erie comes into view. I'm not a patient man, and sitting here, knowing she's down there scared and alone has my insides turning. There's no way I can wait until the veil of darkness gives us enough cover to storm the cabin.

"Let me handle customs when we land," Maverick says as he walks back into the main cabin in full camo and face paint. "They're aware that we're coming, but sneaking in to Canada isn't an easy task and costs a lot of money."

"Pay them anything they want. I want to have that cabin in my sights within the hour, Maverick."

"Phone off, Mr. Forte. No more communication with the outside world, and I want no evidence we were ever here in case everything goes to shit."

Doing as he asks, I turn off my phone and put it in my pocket. There's very little talking as the jet descends through the clouds, finally touching down at a small airport outside Windsor. The customs officials are waiting for us at the gate.

Maverick cuts them off, walking with them about

twenty feet in front of me. I can't hear what they're saying, but when Maverick hands the man a thick envelope and we're quickly left alone, I know we're in. Now there's nothing stopping us from getting to Lauren.

We climb into the black Durango that is waiting for us on the tarmac and take off toward the cabin. The last thing I care about is my life or going to jail; my only concern is getting Lauren away from Trent by any means necessary.

Lauren

Trent sits next to me, holding a gold ring in front of my face. "Do you know what this is?"

I've been on the bed for hours, handcuffed to the headboard, unable to move. My arms are numb to the point of pain, but he's refused my every request to remove the restraints.

"A ring." I wiggle my fingers and wince as it feels like shards of glass are being dragged down my arms.

"Your ring," he whispers.

"My ring?" The pain is pushed to the side by the dread that instantly fills me at his words.

"Do you know why we're here?"

I glance up as his eyes dip to the ring, and he turns it in his fingers. "This is your wedding ring, Lulu. Isn't it beautiful?"

Shock.

Horror.

Numbness.

So many emotions churn through my body that it's hard to breathe.

I want to spit in his face and tell him that he's clearly crazy, but I know it'll do me no good. I'm his captive, chained to a bed we once made love on with no rescue in sight.

There's only one thing I can do to possibly get out of here...I have to play along. Placating Trent and joining his crazy fantasy is the only way I can gain enough freedom to escape the cabin and maybe even with my life.

"It's beautiful," I whisper, almost choking on the lie.

But much like in the boardroom, I have to become a different version of myself. I push aside the little girl who wants to curl into a ball and cry to become someone who steps over the line into his insane fantasy. "I've waited years for you to ask."

A smile flashes across his face, but it quickly disappears. "But what about Antonio?"

I swallow down the bile that's rising in my throat and smile up at the man who deserves nothing short of death. "I was trying to make you jealous, Trent."

It's lunacy, but Trent isn't working with a full deck. Maybe he'll buy the lie and has lost enough rational thought to believe it's true. It's my only hope, and I'm going to stick to the story even if it kills me.

"You've achieved your goal." He reaches down, placing the golden ring on my bare stomach before the palm of his hand rests next to it. "I've been waiting for you to come back to me. I couldn't stand by another minute and watch you drift away."

My bottom sinks into the bed, wanting to escape from his touch, but I go stiff, trying to remain still. "I was never going anywhere. My heart has always belonged to you." The lie comes out easier this time.

He leans forward, pressing his lips to mine. At first, I don't kiss him back, but when his fingers curl painfully into my flesh, I open for him. I almost gag as his tongue sweeps inside my mouth, but the drive to stay alive kicks in and I overcome the sickness.

When he backs away, he smiles as his fingertips caress the tender flesh near my navel. "Tomorrow we'll say our vows before everything ends."

Before everything ends?

"What does that mean?"

He rises from the bed and starts to pace at my side. "We can't go back, Lulu. Our lives there are over. We'll say our vows and enter into the afterlife together."

Every muscle in my body seizes, and I suddenly feel like I'm drowning. His life may be over, but mine has barely begun. I just need to buy enough time for Antonio to find us, if he's already started looking. Even though sometimes I think Antonio's playing me, if he doesn't rescue me, I'll know for sure.

Someone has to have noticed by now that I'm missing. My purse was still in my office when I left to meet Trent. Normally, I would have taken it with me, but I ran out of there in such a hurry, I left it behind. Cassie would have known when she locked up my office at the end of the day. If there's no one else I can count on in my life to realize I'm missing, I still have her.

"We can go back," I whisper, trying to find a way to reason with him.

He walks in longer strides, moving from one end of the cabin to the other like a trapped animal. "We can't. After we say our vows, we must end everything in order to be together forever. I promise to make it painless and easy."

How thoughtful of him to think that I'll be okay with ending my life as long as it's painless. The one thing I know about death is it's never easy. The body fights against the darkness even with no escape. There's nothing easy about it. I've watched someone die before my eyes, and the process is the most horrific thing I've ever witnessed.

"How?" I don't really want to know how he plans to take my life before ending his own, but I need to buy enough time for someone, anyone to find us.

He stops at the foot of the bed and looks down at me with an unnatural calmness. "We'll both fall asleep in each other's arms and never wake up. I can't think of a better way to go. Can you?"

I look down the length of the bed at the man I once thought to be the most brilliant mind on the planet. How easily his genius has transitioned into irrational is absolutely shocking. I should've known something like this could happen after he tried to force himself on me in my office. But who really believes someone could go off the rails in such spectacular fashion as quickly as he did?

"Trent," I whisper, already trying to piece together a way out, but coming up with nothing. "Can you remove the cuffs?"

His fingers curl around the wrought-iron footboard as he gazes down at me. "I don't think it's a good idea."

"But I want to touch you. I'd rather spend tonight making love to you if it'll be our last one together. Can we have one happy night in each other's arms before we die tomorrow?"

He slides onto the bed next to me. "Tell me you love me," he says.

"I love you."

The lies come out easier knowing my life is on the line.

"You promise to be mine forever?"

"I've always been."

I didn't repeat the words he wanted, but I answered in a way that would make him happy. I already said the worst thing I could by saying that I loved him when all I wanted to do was claw his eyeballs out with my bare fingers.

He gazes at me, and neither of us speaks. I pray I'm able to hide my hatred of the man enough so he believes the lies that are falling from my lips on command. When he reaches up and starts to unlock the first handcuff, I take a deep breath and ready myself for what's to come next.

The joy of freedom is quickly replaced by the searing pain as my arms slip downward. I can barely move my arm when the metal slides free from my flesh. I let out a strangled cry as I wiggle my fingers. Trent doesn't respond to my whimpers before moving to the next handcuff and repeating the process.

Even if I wanted to run this very second, I can't. My arms ache with even the slightest movement. I wouldn't make it off the front porch before he'd pull me back in.

"Better?" Trent asks, tossing the key onto the nightstand next to my head.

"Thank you," I bite out through the tears.

He leans forward, brushing his lips against my cheek. "I love you so much, Lulu. I'm sorry if I hurt you, but I didn't know what else to do. I can't lose you."

With my newfound freedom, the lies come easier. I'm one step closer to escaping him. "You could never lose me. I understand why you did what you did. I've been playing hard to get for far too long, and the game's exhausting."

Unable to move my arms, I lie still, letting him touch me even as my skin crawls underneath his fingers. He climbs over me, settling between my legs with the weight of his body on mine and the ring digging into my flesh. "This is all I ever wanted."

"Me too."

We're not talking about the same thing. I want my freedom and his complicity in making it happen. The first chance I have, I'll run for the door and pray I have enough speed to outrun him through the brush that he knows better than I ever will.

Maybe there are campers nearby who will hear my cries before he has a chance to drag me back into the cabin, sealing me away in darkness again.

The pain in my arms starts to wane as the tingling gives way to a dull throb. I wiggle my fingertips, willing the blood back to the very reaches that have been denied circulation for hours. I don't speak as his lips trail down my neck, hovering near my bra strap in a slow, lazy motion.

"You smell just as I remember," he murmurs against my skin. "I need to be inside you."

Tears slide down the side of my face as the realization hits me that no one is coming in time to stop what's about to happen. Maybe asking for my freedom so early wasn't the smartest plan. The very thought of letting Trent inside me, violating my body, has me almost hyperventilating.

"Don't cry, baby. I'll be gentle," he whispers before pulling my bra strap down, exposing my breast.

There's no escape and no pleasure in what's to come. I let my mind wander to Antonio and our time on the island. My mind drifts away to the beach, the water lapping at my feet, and the feel of his skin on mine.

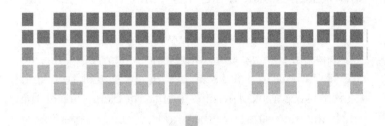

Chapter 4

Antonio

My body almost vibrates across the ground as we approach the cabin. We covered the few miles from the main road to the cabin in under a half hour and barely broke a sweat in the damp, cold spring air of Canada. Maverick has stopped speaking, opting for hand signals so we're not overheard by Trent.

He's in full-on commando mode, harkening back to his days in the military, and has his gun out in front of him ready to shoot anything that walks in front of us. My finger is itching to pull the trigger, but I'd prefer to hit Trent right between the eyes so Lauren never has to look over her shoulder again and wonder if the madman is after her.

Maverick uses his two fingers to motion between his eyes and the cabin. I haven't a clue what he means, but my limited knowledge from action movies leads me to believe he's going to check the surroundings. He holds his palm out to me and points to the ground.

I nod because I don't know what else to do before he wanders off. I suppose he wants me to stay put while he checks out the cabin and searches for any sign of Trent and Lauren. I keep track of his movement as he blends in with the brush and moves through the woods, circling the perimeter of the cabin. Every few seconds, I let my eyes drift toward the windows, praying for any sign that Lauren's alive.

Within a minute, Maverick's back at my side. He starts motioning with his hand, but now I can't even fathom a guess at what all the little movements mean. "Speak, Maverick," I whisper. "I don't know what this means." I repeat his finger motions, or as near to what he had done as I can, back to him.

He stands as close to me as he possibly can without becoming physically attached to me and places his mouth next to my ear. "I got a visual from the side window. They're in there, sir."

I squint, trying to see anything through the front windows, but it's just a wall with a window to the back. "What did you see?"

"They're on the bed."

I turn my head slightly, and my lips tighten along with every muscle in my body. "Is she hurt?"

"Couldn't tell."

The fact that Trent has her on the bed and is probably

touching her against her will has my blood boiling. I'm ready to choke the life out of him with my bare hands, the law be damned.

"I can't wait another two hours for darkness. We don't have time to waste. We need to move."

"Let me get one more visual and make sure he's preoccupied before we bust down the front door."

"Get the visual, but I'm going in either way," I tell him, done with waiting around for the sun to set.

It won't change the outcome. Either way, we're going in, and if someone dies, I sure as hell don't plan on it being me. We have the element of surprise on our side. Trent probably assumes he's covered his tracks enough that it would take us days to find him, but he underestimated my ability to track down the woman I love.

Maverick backs away and gives me a quick nod before jogging back to the side of the house so quietly I don't even hear his footsteps. The man had to have been a beast during his military days and has probably killed more people than I'd want to know. I'm happy he's on my side and not working for the enemy.

I can't take my eyes off the cabin, wondering what's happening inside and if Lauren's okay. Maverick said they were on the bed, and I know Trent's touching her. I can't imagine the mental pain she's feeling, trying to reason with a deranged lunatic.

Maverick's large frame creates a shadow around me as he jogs back to my side. "We're good to go. I'll go in first and bust the door down before taking Trent out. After he's out of the picture, you can come in and grab Lauren, sir."

I stare up at him, playing the scenario through my head. I can't think of a better idea. "We're just going to run up there?"

He moves close again, trying to keep his husky, deep voice as low as possible. "No. We're going to take it slow. I don't need a lot of space to knock that shitty wood door off its hinges. Just a swift kick of my boot, and it'll be done. I'll have him on the floor before he has a chance to even react on instinct."

"I'll be right behind you."

He walks slowly, too slowly for my liking, but he's in charge even if I'm the one signing his checks. With careful attention, we step around fallen branches and anything that could cause an unnatural sound before making our way to the corner of the cabin. As if he weighs nothing, Maverick walks across the planks of the porch, ducking underneath every window to avoid detection. I stay near the corner, knowing my limits and not willing to risk Lauren's life just so I can be glued to Maverick's back.

He motions to me, holding up three fingers.

Two.

One.

He lifts his leg off the ground and rears back before thrusting forward with so much force that the door busts into tiny pieces under the impact.

Lauren

I turn my head to the side and stare at the old brown lamp on the nightstand. If I could move over a few more inches, I could probably touch it, but I wouldn't be near enough to wrap my fingers around the base. It's the only thing close enough with enough weight to knock Trent out if I hit him at just the right angle.

"You feel so good," Trent says, moving down the middle of my chest with his body weight pinning me to the mattress.

I touch his arm, sliding my fingernails gently across his skin as I make my way up to his shoulder. "You too."

He murmurs his appreciation as I swallow down my fear. I drop my hand from his shoulder, placing it near my face. I writhe against the bed, pretending I'm enjoying the feel of his lips against my flesh. I've never been good at faking it, but Trent's too busy with his own pleasure to notice.

His erection presses into my leg as his mouth skates down the right side of my rib cage. I inch my fingers toward the nightstand, straining to touch the metal base.

The weight of Trent's body lessens, and I freeze. "What are you doing?"

My eyes dart to his and widen when I realize he's staring at my hand. "I have a cramp. I'm just stretching." Fuck. I thought I was moving so slowly that he wouldn't notice.

He pulls my body over, making it impossible to reach the lamp now. "I'm sorry I kept you chained up for so long." He covers my shoulder with his hand, massaging it roughly.

I grit my teeth through the soreness that his fingers make more painful. He smiles down at me as he works his way toward my neck. "Better?"

"Yes."

This wasn't how I thought my life would end. I planned on working until I was so old that the only suits that would fit me would come from a senior clothing store and require elastic. I figured I'd move from the boardroom right into an assisted living facility to live out the rest of my years watching episodes of reality television while I ate food that had been sent through a food processor to prevent my toothless mouth from choking. Even though it's depressing, that vision is better than the one of my dying at the hands of my ex-lover.

My eyes burn as tears start to form. Every little spark of hope fades from my body as I realize there's no escaping the fate Trent has determined on my behalf. I gaze up at the ceiling, staring at the tiny black cracks in the beams above my head. I try to lose myself in the blackness as Trent's lips and hands explore my body and I'm powerless to stop him.

He starts to pull down his pants, and I know what's coming, but I don't plan on helping him in any way. I remain motionless and distant as he pulls at the waistband of my underwear.

I close my eyes, repeating the serenity prayer to myself as he slides the lace down my legs. My skin crawls under his touch, and I close my eyes and regret the lies I said earlier that put me in this situation.

Just as the material crosses my ankles, the door smashes open, causing us both to jump. Trent's on his feet, pants halfway down his legs and not ready for company.

A beast of a man dressed in camouflage and black face paint bursts through the doorway with his gun drawn.

Trent growls, lurching at the man who's easily a foot taller and no match for him physically. Before Trent can get within five feet of the man, there's a single shot fired.

I cover my ears and let out a scream as Trent stumbles backward, gripping his chest. Blood oozes between his fingers, sliding down his chest as he falls to the floor. His mouth is open as he gasps for air, but no sound comes from his lips. The same lips that moments ago had assaulted my flesh.

I should be horrified at the scene before me, but even if the man who pulled the trigger is here to kill me too, at least I had the satisfaction of watching Trent die first. I'm not afraid to die. Everyone I've ever loved has taken the journey before me. I always allowed myself to believe in something more than what we have on this planet and in this body. I dreamed of the day I'd wrap my arms around my father again and be cradled by my mother. I just didn't want it to be at the hands of the worthless person dying before my very eyes.

"Ms. Bradley," the man says softly with the gun down at his side.

I drag my eyes away from Trent's lifeless body as a hand pushes the man out of the way. My heart leaps as Antonio moves my way, wearing the same outfit and makeup, looking completely out of place.

"Antonio?" I whisper as tears spill down my cheeks. My heart skips out a rhythm faster than it had moments ago when I thought I was going to die.

He wraps his powerful arms around me, holding my face tightly against his chest. "Lauren. Oh God." He rocks me gently and kisses the top of my head as I melt into him.

"You're here."

I wonder if I'm dreaming and maybe my imagination went off the rails somewhere after Trent slipped my panties off my legs.

When Antonio pulls back and his hands touch my face, those blue eyes bore into me, and I know he's real. "I'd move heaven and earth to find you."

I smile through my tears, but they fall harder knowing I didn't dream this. The headline in the newspaper won't be about my murder-suicide death at the hands of my ex-lover and Interstellar employee.

This man, my one-time enemy, who had so quickly stolen my heart, has now become my savior from the darkness. "You're here," I repeat.

"Sir, take Ms. Bradley outside."

Antonio wraps the blanket from the bottom of the bed around my body before lifting me into his arms. I curl into him and close my eyes, feeling that I'm finally safe and that the nightmare is over.

As he carries me toward the door, I take a final glance at Trent's body sprawled out on the floor, covered in blood that's now pooled underneath him.

"Don't look," Antonio whispers.

He doesn't understand that I've seen a person die before. I've watched as someone has taken their last breath. I held my father's hand as he gasped for air with his glassy eyes staring into the nothingness until his body gave out. That moment was devastating. Watching someone you're not ready to let go of cease to exist is more than any person should have to bear.

Seeing Trent doing the same has no effect on me. After the hell he put me through, I pray that every last breath is painful and impossible.

Clutching Antonio's shirt, I let the tears flow. Not tears of sadness or fear, but those of utter joy and relief. Even though I reached for the lamp, I didn't know how I'd find my way out of the wilderness. Trent knew every nook and cranny of the woods surrounding the cabin, and I wouldn't have gotten far before he pulled me back in.

Antonio leans forward, holding my body against his as he sits down on the edge of the porch. "Are you hurt?" he asks, lifting the blanket enough to see my skin.

"I'm okay."

And I am.

I'm better than okay. I'm alive and free.

The hours of mental anguish from being at the hands of a lunatic will eventually fade. Knowing he's dead, will make it possible for me to not have to relive it at every turn. I won't have to sit through a trial and face the man who tried to steal my future along with my life.

"Oh God. Did he..." Antonio's voice trails off, and I can hear the pain in his words.

I want there to be no questions about what happened in that cabin. Trent did not rape me. He would have if he were given the chance, and most likely, I would've been powerless to stop him. But he never got that far because Antonio saved me.

I lift my eyes to Antonio, pushing my head off his chest and cradling his cheek in my hand. "He didn't. You came before he could..." I choke on what could've happened if Antonio hadn't rescued me when he did.

The man walks out of the cabin, turning his phone over in his palm with his gun stowed in the holster. "He's dead. My men will come handle his body before nightfall."

"Thank you, Maverick."

I smile at the man towering over us who Antonio calls Maverick. "Thank you," I whisper and wipe away the tears on my cheek. "I don't know how to thank you two enough."

"I'll grab the car so we can get back to the States before we run into any issues," he says with a handsome smile.

I don't ask any questions. I don't want to know about his men and how they're going to handle Trent's remains. I couldn't care less if they leave him in the open wilderness and let the wildlife peck away at his flesh until he's nothing more than bones.

For the first time since that bastard wrapped his hands around my throat, I feel like I can breathe. Being cradled in Antonio's arms, listening to the steady beat of his heart, I let the exhaustion pull me under as he carries me down the dirt road.

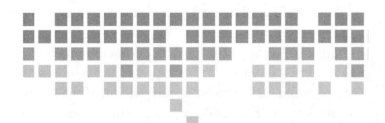

Chapter 5

Antonio

I regret not pulling the trigger myself. Lauren looked so far away when we entered the cabin, like a lost soul waiting for death. She barely blinked and spoke in a voice so unlike her own. My heart ached the moment I laid eyes on her. I thought I was prepared for anything, but seeing her like that...so lifeless...had knocked the wind clear out of me.

Standing in the doorway, I watch her carefully as she sleeps. Her long brown hair is messy and wet, crowning her face as she lies in the middle of the bed. She ate on the plane and wanted nothing more than a hot bath once we returned to her place. My team had done a great job in the cleaning of her apartment and had been able to replace almost everything that had been damaged.

My phone vibrates in my hand, and I glance down. Maverick's men in Canada gave the all clear. I didn't want any details. As long as there would be no trace of Trent's death leading back to Lauren and me, I didn't care what they did with him.

"Antonio." Lauren's soft voice carries through the room, washing over me.

I push the phone back into my pocket and make my way to her. "You're safe." I've repeated those words to her a hundred times since I carried her out of the cabin. I'll keep saying them until she believes them too.

"What are you doing?" She winces through a stretch, looking entirely too small and fragile in the large king-size bed.

Sliding in next to her, I pull her against my side, resting my head above hers. My fingers tangle in her hair as I stroke the delicate skin on her neck where it meets her hairline. "Just checking on you. You really should rest."

"How bad is it?"

I gaze down at her. "How bad is what?"

She pulls away and pushes herself upright as my hands fall from her body. "The damage to my company."

"There's none, Lauren."

Her stare hardens. "None?"

I shake my head and sit next to her. "I made sure everything remained quiet."

"Someone had to ask questions."

"Cassie handled it."

"How?"

"I'll place a few calls, and tomorrow we'll pick up the pieces. But tonight, I want you to rest. You're safe and alive, and that's all that matters."

Work is the least important thing at the moment. I don't care if Interstellar or Cozza crashes and burns as long as she's okay. So many horrible things could've happened, and it could've been her dead on the floor of that cabin instead of Trent. I know how precious and short life is, and I will never waste another opportunity to seize the day.

"You know how important work is to me."

"I'll get an update about what happened today to ease your mind, but everything else can wait until tomorrow. Yes?"

She twists her lips but nods anyway, mimicking my movements. I'll settle for nothing less. After the last twenty-four hours being the most hellish I'd ever experienced, the last thing I want to do is worry about something that is being handled by our employees.

"There's a doctor coming over to check you out." Her eyes widen, and she's about to protest when I cover her lips with my finger. "Humor me, will you?" Right on time, there's a knock on the door. "Just be nice to the man, and he'll be done quickly."

She rolls her eyes before easing back against the headboard with her arms folded. "Show him in."

I leave her room, but not before looking back over my shoulder and taking another look. I haven't been able to stop staring at her, needing to remind myself that she's real. I show the doctor to her room, closing the door and leaving them alone before placing a call to Carlino for an update.

"We missed you today," he says, twisting the dagger he'd like to stick in my back a little more. "It was a very eventful day."

"Just give me the details. I'm not in the mood for your games," I bite out as I pace through the kitchen and far enough away from her bedroom so she won't overhear.

"Josh will be presenting the terms to the board and shareholders tomorrow. He called an emergency meeting. It looks like Interstellar has finally seen the light."

"Don't fuck this up, Carlino. I'll be at the Interstellar board meeting."

"I can do it," he says, but with him, there's always a reason he offers to do anything. He's not a selfless man. He doesn't know it, but his time at Cozza is done, and he won't be continuing with the newly formed company.

"I'll. Be. There," I say again and hang up before he can say another word.

Lauren

Antonio strides back into the room after showing the doctor out. I'm thankful I don't have to be alone tonight. Normally, I like my time to myself, but I can't fathom another second without Antonio by my side. I want to go back to those days at the beach. There was so much serenity as we stared up at the stars. Although things seemed so complicated then, I'd give anything to go back.

"Everything go okay?" Antonio asks as he climbs into the bed next to me.

I turn on my side, resting my head against his chest and listen to the steady beat of his heart underneath me. "He said I'm fine and that I can return to work tomorrow."

"Take one day off, Lauren. I beg you."

I slide my hand up his chest, resting it on his cheek as I stare down the length of him. "I need to get back to normal, Antonio. I can't lie here all day tomorrow and think about what happened."

The last thing I need is downtime. Lying in this bed, staring at the ceiling, will just cause the memories of the cabin to come rushing back, slamming into me again. I want to forget. I want to push it as far out of my memory as possible.

"Just one day is all I ask. Cassie can keep you updated, and you can take calls from bed. But don't rush back into the office."

"Why?" I twirl my finger in the back of his hair just behind his ear.

"I'd hate for you to break down in front of people. Give your mind a day to rest before you walk back into the lion's den."

I hate to admit that he's right. I can't afford to have a mental breakdown in front of my coworkers or the board of directors. If Cassie covered my tracks, explaining why I turned into a crying mess will have people asking more questions than I can afford to answer.

"Fine," I say, curling into his body and covering his legs with mine. I'm holding on to him tightly, cradling him like he's a security blanket. "I'll do it for you."

"For us," he corrects as he runs his warm palm down my back in long, languid strokes.

I still can't fathom an "us" in the future. We're competitors by nature and circumstance. After leaving the island, I let myself believe for a moment that it was possible, but it's just a whimsical fantasy I let myself buy into.

"Stay with me tonight?" I whisper into his chest.

He flattens his palm against my back, pulling me closer as he settles into the mattress. "Close your eyes, mi amore."

I let my eyes close, content in his arms, surrounded by his warmth and strength. The sound of his heart and the softness of his fingertips skating across my skin lulls me into a sleep like I haven't experienced in years.

***

When I open my eyes and roll over, I blink a few times and stare at the clock. I blink again, figuring I'm still dreaming. Ten. I bolt straight up, and my arms begin to throb. For a moment, I think I'm late to work, until the events of the last few days slam straight into me.

Trent.

The cabin.

Blood.

I can barely control my breathing as the visuals flash through my mind, and every emotion I've felt since he choked me hits me all at once. I cradle my face in my hands and let myself feel everything. The fear. The sadness. The shock. The joy.

I will not allow myself to wallow in self-pity. I've never been a victim, and I don't plan on starting now. I let myself cry as I sit here alone for these few minutes. That's all I have in me to give to a man like Trent and what he put me through. It's in the past and completely behind me. I refuse to dwell on what happened for too long because I'm unwilling to lose who I am at my core.

I'm Lauren Bradley. First female CEO of one of the biggest aerospace companies in the world. I'm a force unto myself, and no man, not even Antonio Forte, can stop me from achieving my goal.

Repeating the words like a mantra, I sit up a little straighter and wipe away the tears. In the quietness of the room, I hear Antonio's voice, distant and muffled.

Pushing myself up, I pad across the carpet, trying to hear his conversation, but the door garbles the sound too much. Slowly, I turn the handle and try to avoid making a sound before I tiptoe down the hallway toward his voice.

"Is it done?" he asks a man on the phone.

He's pacing the kitchen in his polished black suit and red tie. He looks so handsome as he rakes his hand through his hair, stopping in front of the floor-to-ceiling windows and looking out across the city.

"We'll call a press conference soon enough. Just sit tight. I'm about to head into the office," Antonio states with his back to me.

I plaster my body against the wall and grip the cold surface for support. I feel like someone has sucker-punched me right in the stomach.

How could Antonio move forward without me? If he truly wanted something more with me, why would he lie straight to my face?

It's not the first time he's lied.

He still hasn't told me who the mole was that sold us out to Cozza in the first place, even though he signed the contract which clearly stated he would reveal the name after our weekend had concluded.

I walk toward the bedroom, my legs shaking as I use the walls for support. Once inside, I close the door before crawling back into bed and covering my face with the blanket.

All the men in my life are turning out to be two-faced. They're liars and psychopaths, and I fell for both of them.

"Lauren," Antonio calls out as he gently knocks on the door.

I close my eyes, unwilling to look at him. I do what I did in the dark room at Trent's cabin, I pretend to be asleep. The door opens, and for a minute, I hold my breath, waiting for him to walk closer.

Go away.

I'm sick of being let down by the men in my life. The only male I could ever depend on was my father, and he's no longer here to hold my hand and guide me.

When the door closes and Antonio's footsteps grow quieter as he walks down the hallway, I finally allow myself to take a deep breath and sprawl out across the bed.

"Fuck him," I whisper.

How dare he do this to me?

I kick the blankets off in a fury, ready to face the world.

Chapter 6

Antonio

Even though I'm sitting in the boardroom surrounded by a table full of the top executives at Cozza, I can't focus on the discussion no matter how hard I try. I hate that I left Lauren today. I should've stayed and at least waited for her to wake up.

What kind of asshole leaves his girl behind after the events of the last few days because he has to go into work? Me. As the CEO of Cozza, I have the ability to leave everything in the hands of my team, but the merger with Interstellar is too important for me not to watch it play out.

As part of the merger, I want to ensure that Lauren is given the highest position. She's earned it and deserves it above everyone else. With the completion of the

Mercury engine, no one's going to disagree. I needed to come in to make sure that Carlino or Josh didn't find a way to inch her out of a job she's clearly earned.

"Who will head the new company?" Carlino asks right on cue.

My eyes dart to him and narrow as I lean back in my chair, waiting to hear what everyone else has to say before I give my opinion.

"I think Mr. Forte should still be CEO," Mr. Fiorentino, the oldest and most respected member, states. "That would make the most sense."

"Yes," Piper McKay, our most recent addition, adds as he twirls his pen between his fingertips. "He has the most experience and has brought Cozza to the top and maintained our position there for more than a decade."

When Piper joined the board of Cozza, I figured he'd just sit around the table nodding, without adding anything to the conversation. He received his position through his father, the CEO before me. After he graduated from Northwestern with a degree in business, his father felt he should get his feet wet at Cozza.

Carlino leans forward and clears his throat. "Maybe it's time we allow someone else to take the new company in an even bigger direction."

I smile at Carlino because he's so predictable. I knew the man would take any opportunity to stab me in the back. He's baggage we can no longer afford to carry. If Lauren's to head the new company, he's going to be out on his ass before the ink is dry on the new deal.

"Ludicrous," Fiorentino barks. "What you're suggesting would be a quick way for this company's stock to tank as soon as the merger is complete. We need stability in the newly formed company, not a complete shake-up."

"I have just as much experience as Mr. Forte, and I have worked by his side for years. I could do the job just as well, if not better, than he does. Plus, I don't have any distractions, unlike Mr. Forte, and I could devote all of my time to Cozza Interstellar."

I crack my knuckles before resting my elbows on the table. "You're right about one thing, Carlino." I take a deep breath, and every person around the table gawks at me. "There should be someone new as the CEO of Cozza Interstellar, but it shouldn't be you."

"That's bullshit, Antonio, and you know it."

I smirk. "What I know, Carlino—" His name slides off my tongue as if I just hurled an insult in his direction. "Is that you'd sell out your mother, not to mention your CEO and this company, if it meant you'd get a higher position. You're a fame whore."

He rises to his feet and slams his fist against the table, causing all the water glasses to bounce. "I am not."

"You're the one who went in search of insider information and paid off someone at Interstellar against my orders."

He's still standing, hovering over the table like a caged beast. The vein that runs down the middle of his forehead pulses and looks like it's ready to burst. "I made this deal happen. Whether you like how I achieved the goal isn't in question. The future of this company is at stake, and maybe you're not the man we need to bring us into the future."

"I couldn't agree more." I rise from my seat at the head of the table and walk behind the board members. Moving slowly, I touch the top of each seat as I pass. "I no longer wish to be CEO of Cozza Interstellar. I've taken the company to the top, and it's still my main priority to keep us there. But there's someone else who has more vision and, frankly, balls to take us in the right direction and keep us rising for many years to come."

Carlino's eyes bulge, and that vein gets a little closer to exploding.

I smile at him as I walk past and keep my slow, steady pace around the table. "Moving forward, I'd like to take on the role of COO of the combined company and be second-in-command to the new CEO. Based on everything I know about this business from my years of experience and documented success, the new CEO needs to be a visionary."

"Mr. Forte, you have been our visionary for more years than I've been a member of this board. What makes you think you're not the best person for the job?" Piper asks.

"I could do the job, Piper. Without a doubt, I could remain CEO and maintain the greatness of this company. But I think someone else will help us achieve things I never thought possible."

"Don't say it." Carlino bares his teeth.

I shake my head. "I'd like to put Lauren Bradley up for consideration as CEO of Cozza Interstellar as soon as the new company is formed. I'd willingly take the second-in-command role and work side by side with Ms. Bradley, a true visionary, to catapult us into the future."

"He's sleeping with her," Carlino blurts out in front of the entire room.

The look of shock on the board members' faces matches my own. "My personal feelings for Ms. Bradley have nothing to do with my decision."

Piper's fingers stop moving, and the pen falls to the table. "So, you are sleeping with her?"

"Whatever has or hasn't happened in my personal life has no bearing on my decision. Ms. Bradley did something no one else has done." I look down the table at the other members and grip the top of my chair. "She developed an engine that doesn't require fuel. She changed a system that had remained the same for almost one hundred years. She did something we've never been able to do in the time since Cozza began more than fifty years ago. She's the one who should lead us forward because of her vision."

Mr. Fiorentino rubs his forehead and lets out a loud, exasperated sigh. "We have many things to consider before this deal goes through. We'll take all information into consideration before we reach an agreement, but Ms. Bradley has shown that she has the ability to lead the new corporation. With you by her side, I don't see where we can go wrong."

"Agreed," Piper says, followed by the other less talkative members sitting around the table.

"I will only step down if Ms. Bradley is given the position. Then I would resume the role of COO, which I held previously."

"Where does that leave me?" Carlino asks, practically seething.

"I heard Boeing is looking for some help," I reply with a smirk that isn't missed by Carlino or the other members. "We need to have a team who has the company's best interests at heart, not their own."

"I won't stand for this, Antonio. I'll make sure that you and your side piece..."

"This is the attitude I referred to. I didn't hear a word about Cozza in those last two sentences, just 'I.' This company is bigger and more important than one person."

Carlino stalks out of the room, slamming the door behind him as the board members watch in horror.

"I'm very sorry you had to witness that, ladies and gentlemen. I thank you for your time today and for considering my request to place Ms. Bradley in charge of Cozza Interstellar. Remember, her board must agree to the merger too in order for the deal to go through. I'm sure they'd feel more comfortable knowing she would retain her position. If the deal falls through, they'll become the new number one as soon as their engine gets into full production. Now if you'll excuse me, I need to attend to a few things."

I leave them all to talk amongst themselves and step into the hallway to call Lauren. When there's no answer, I call Cassie.

"Ms. Bradley's office," she answers.

"Have you heard from Ms. Bradley today?"

"She's here, sir, but I'm under strict orders not to put your calls through."

"Why?"

"I don't know. She muttered something about the

merger when she walked in, and now she's meeting with Mr. Goldman."

"Fuck," I hiss, gripping my cracked screen so tightly that the glass digs into my fingertips. "I'll be right there."

"Good luck," she says before she hangs up.

The last time Lauren and I discussed business, before she disappeared, the deal had just been placed before her. She hadn't even had a chance to give her blessing before Trent ripped her away from her life. And I put Mr. Goldman and Carlino in charge of everything without taking into account how she'd feel about everything.

I should've been honest with her. This morning before I left, I should've told her that the merger was moving forward and explained how I planned to make her the new CEO and that I'd be her second-in-command.

I fucked up, and now I have to make things right.

Lauren

I'm tapping my pen against the pad of paper as I stare at Josh. It's the only thing I can do to stop myself from lunging across the desk and wrapping my hands around his throat until I choke the life out of him.

"I did it for the company," he says, nervously rubbing his palms against the armrests of the chair. "I swear."

He can repeat that a million times, and I'd never believe it. Josh is out for number one, just like everyone else in this building. In a way, so am I, but it's to fulfill my father's dream and not to gain corporate fame and wealth.

I point at the door without looking him in the eyes.

"Get out."

"Lauren."

"Out, Josh."

Josh pauses in the doorway, but he leaves when I don't look in his direction.

I have nothing left. I don't even have the energy to yell. I'm spent from the last few days, and Josh's and Antonio's betrayals just add to the sting of Trent's heinous act.

"Ma'am." Cassie's voice comes through the speaker on my desktop telephone. "Tara's on the phone for you."

"Put her through, Cassie." I lift the receiver to my ear because I know Tara's going to be Tara, therefore loud and probably spewing profanity like a late-night comic.

"Jesus Christ," she says before I've even had a chance to say hello.

"What?" My voice is defensive even though I knew she was going to give me an earful as soon as I picked up the phone.

"Last night you told me you were taking the day off. Now you're at fucking work? Dude," she groans loudly. "What the hell is wrong with you?"

"I've been gone too long as it is. I couldn't take another day."

"Bullshit," she barks. "You're a workaholic. You were kidnapped, for shit's sake. The last place you should be is in that hostile work environment."

"It's not hostile."

"Babe, it's like the Hunger Games without the shiny weapons. I'm going to call Antonio."

"No!" Every muscle in my body tenses.

"Why not?"

Ugh. The last thing I want is to have this conversation with Tara. There's too much on my plate to explain everything that happened this morning.

"I can't trust him, Tara. Leave it at that."

"I don't know what messed-up shit is going on in that pretty little head of yours, but the man tracked you down in another country and rescued you from a lunatic."

"I know."

What else is there to say? He did that, but that doesn't mean he did it for the right reasons. It doesn't matter that he saved my life when he's trying to ruin my company and my career in the process.

"Besides me, he's probably the only person you can trust, Lauren."

"I gotta run. I'm late for a meeting."

She starts to say something, but I hang up before she gets more than a few words out of her mouth. I'm well aware of everything Antonio has done for me, and I'm grateful, but that doesn't mean he's earned the right to have free rein over my entire life or my company.

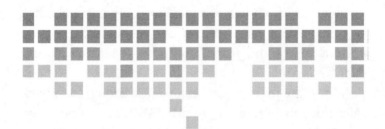

Chapter 7

Antonio

"I wouldn't go in there," Cassie says, stepping in front of me just as I reach for the handle of Lauren's office door.

I stare down at her, trying to control my anger that's about to boil over. "Cassie," I say, trying to plaster a fake smile on my face. "I know you're doing what you think is best for Lauren, but she shouldn't be here right now."

"I know." Her lips purse, and she takes a deep breath. "I told her that already, Mr. Forte, but she told me to keep my opinions to myself."

I rest my hands on her shoulders and give them a light squeeze. "Let me just talk to her for a minute. Maybe I can talk some sense into her."

"She gave me strict orders not to let you anywhere near her office."

"So, walk away, and I'll let myself in."

Cassie nibbles on the corner of her bottom lip, staring up at me. "I don't know."

"Just go," I tell her because I'm going into the office even if I have to pick Cassie up and set her aside. No one is going to keep me from Lauren, even her tiny pit bull of an assistant.

"I'm going to trust you because you brought her back safe. But this is a one-time deal, Mr. Forte. I never go against Ms. Bradley's wishes, but I will this once because she shouldn't be here today."

"Thank you, Cassie." I smile, giving her shoulders another light squeeze. "I promise you won't regret it."

She hesitates for a moment before she backs up, keeping her eyes locked with mine. "I won't be far," she says.

I knock lightly before opening the door. "Lauren." I gaze at her as she sits at her desk with the sunlight streaming through the windows, bathing her in light.

She's out of her seat quickly, walking in my direction with narrowed eyes. "Get out."

"I'm not leaving."

She tries to slap me, but I grab her hand and pull her into an embrace. She wiggles against me, but I don't break the hold. "You shouldn't be here."

She glares at me as if I'm the monster that kidnapped her. "You're not my father, Antonio."

"We talked about this. It's not good for you to be here so soon."

Her stare turns icy. "It's hard to steal my company when I'm here, isn't it?" She steps back as soon as I drop my arms. "I always knew you'd stab me in the back."

Her words rock me to the core, but I step forward, unable to put more space between us. "You can't be serious. I've done nothing to you, Lauren. You need to come home."

She crosses her arms in front of her chest, raising a shoulder as she glares at me. "I heard you on the phone this morning, and I've spoken with Josh."

She steps back as I move closer. "I didn't stab you in the back."

"The merger is going through. You did it without even asking for my thoughts."

She has a point. I may have gotten ahead of myself, but the board was pushing for the deal to move faster. With everything she'd been through, I thought I was doing what was best for both of us. I thought I was doing what was best for everyone, but clearly, I've been selfish.

"The boards could no longer wait, and I thought it was in your best interest if I handled everything myself."

She jerks her head backward as her eyes widen. "Did I miss the memo where you speak on my behalf?"

I rub the back of my neck and feel like the biggest asshole in the history of the world. Even if I wanted her to rest, I should've at least kept her in the loop about everything that was happening. "I'm sorry," I say, bringing my eyes to hers. "I didn't want you to worry about anything."

As soon as the words leave my mouth, I wish I could reel them back in. I'm not sure I've ever said anything so stupid to a woman or a business partner before. How could I think that handling everything on her behalf would give her peace of mind?

I drop onto the couch just behind me and lean back. My eyes travel up the length of her body. Fierce and beautiful in her anger directed at me, she rocks back and forth, her fury coming across in her movements and her eyes.

"Listen," I say, motioning for her to come to me, but she shakes her head and squares her shoulders. I drag my hands through my hair, trying to figure out what to say next that won't have her tossing me out on my ass in the next minute.

"The deal is in motion now, Antonio. There's nothing you can say to stop it. Everything I've worked so hard for all these years is ruined."

"That's not true."

Everything I've done is for her. There is no one else in the world I'd give up my place in the company for except her, but she has no idea about the inner workings and what I've already set into motion.

"It is. You rush in to rescue me and then rip away my life. You should've just left me in that cabin with Trent."

I rise to my feet and stalk toward her, filled with rage. "Shut your mouth." I grip the back of her neck and bring her lips to mine. "I'm saving our companies and our careers, Lauren."

Her rough, fast breathing matches mine as she glares at me. "You lie," she growls.

I stare into her fiery eyes as her warm, sweet breath cascades across my lips. My hold on her neck loosens as my fingers tangle in the hair at the nape of her neck. "Everything I did is for you."

Her hands push against my chest as she struggles to get out of my grip. "Let me go."

"I won't." I glower at her until she stops trying to break free from my hold. "Not until you listen to me."

She goes rigid in my arms and purses her lips. "Talk."

I lean forward, pressing my lips against hers. I need the connection. I need her to remember what we had just a few days ago, or hell, what we had before she overheard my conversation this morning and thought I was still trying to steal her company. My tongue slides across hers, and they tangle together. Anger fuels our kiss with each passing second as her fingers dig into the skin at my neck. When I finally pull away, her breathing matches mine as we gasp for air.

"Don't do that again," she says before pulling her swollen bottom lip between her teeth.

I wrap an arm around her back, solidifying my hold on her. "You're mine, Lauren, and I'm yours. I'll do what's necessary to make you happy, no matter the cost."

"You can't kiss me, profess your love, and then rip away my dream, Antonio. You're not playing fair."

Leaning forward, I place my face in the crook of her neck and close my eyes. Even in her anger, I feel at peace. "I'm not ripping anything away. I have made it very clear that you're to be the CEO of the new company."

She jerks away and out of my hold. Her eyes search my face, trying to find the lie in my truth. "But..."

"I'm giving up my position for you."

Lauren

I stumble backward, speechless.

I couldn't possibly have heard him correctly. He's giving up his position at the company for me?

I blink repeatedly and stare at him again. The Antonio Forte I knew, the notorious asshole and CEO of Cozza who is spoken about in whispers, wouldn't give up his seat so quickly.

"Why?"

He drags his hand through his beautiful, dark hair, but he keeps his eyes on mine. "It's the right thing to do."

I rest my bottom on the desk behind me to avoid falling over. My body's tingling, and everything feels so surreal in this moment, almost as if I'm dreaming. "When have you ever done something because it's right?"

He moves forward, stepping between my feet. He touches my chin, forcing me to look at him. "I do when you're involved."

My heart flutters as he says the words. I open my mouth and close it again, unsure of what to say. I can't figure out why he'd do that. It shouldn't matter that I'm involved because a few days together doesn't make up for the career he's spent his lifetime building. "I mean nothing, Antonio."

"You mean everything." He grips my hips as he steps forward, and I lose my breath. The look in his eyes says everything without his uttering a word. There's an intensity behind the ocean blue that I haven't seen before.

I flatten my palm against his chest and press myself against him. "I…" I don't know what to say. I'm rarely at a loss for words, especially when it comes to Interstellar, but Antonio has knocked the wind right out of me. "How? We've barely spent time together."

I'd be lying if I didn't admit, at least to myself, that I feel the same way about him. The weekend alone with him changed how I view him. He's not the monster I thought based on the way he's portrayed by others in our industry. Yes, he's difficult, unforgiving when he's going after something he wants, but there's more to him than meets the eye.

"Lauren," he says as he brushes the backs of his fingers against my cheek tenderly. I move into his touch. "I know you don't believe in fate, but I do."

You're mine, and I'm yours.

I swallow hard as my heart starts to beat faster, and the words he spoke moments ago repeat in my head. No one has ever said them to me. Not even Trent in all his jealous insanity. Antonio said the words with so much tenderness and fierceness that I could almost feel them caress my soul.

"After our night together, I couldn't get you out of my head, and I drove myself crazy. I thought I'd never see you again, but then you were placed in front of me. Even though we were enemies, I couldn't imagine not touching you at least one more time." He closes the space between us and pulls me forward, pressing our bodies together. "I had a grand plan for our weekend on the island, but the first night, it went to shit. I couldn't use you. You're more beautiful than any star in the sky."

Tears start to form in my eyes as he speaks. My mind is telling me to keep fighting and not to fall for his romantic words, but my heart and the feel of him against my skin make me want to cave.

His gaze captivates me. "I couldn't go through with it. When we lay on the beach and stared into the heavens, I decided I wanted more from you than a weekend. I've searched all my life for someone, Lauren, and never found anyone special before you strolled into my bar."

"You walked into my bar," I correct him with a tiny smile.

The seriousness on his face eases as he grins and shakes his head. "Before we left the island, I knew I'd do anything in my power to make you happy and keep you by my side. And when you were kidnapped, I almost went out of my mind." He pauses, and the seriousness returns. "I would've killed Trent with my bare hands to save you." He brushes a strand of hair behind my ear before his finger slides down my face, tracing my jaw. "There isn't anything I wouldn't do for you."

I stare into his eyes, still in disbelief. "But giving up your company..."

He places his finger over my lips. "You're the right person to lead us into the future, and I'll be at your side the entire time."

I wrap my hands around his neck and fight back the tears. "I don't know what to say."

"Just say yes." He smiles.

"Yes," I say quickly. "But only if you're at my side."

"There's no place I'd rather be," he says and pauses before his hand that had been resting on my hip slides under my ass. "Unless you're naked, then I want you under me."

I laugh softly and lean forward, pressing my lips to his. Closing my eyes, I forget the anger that filled me just minutes ago.

Like an ass, I had everything all wrong.

Antonio wasn't trying to steal Interstellar from me. I'd grown so paranoid and let my assumptions about him lead me astray. I needed to remember that the man in the elegant business suit was the same man with the sexy smile and sun-kissed skin on the island. The same man who held my hand and stared up at the night sky for hours without uttering one complaint.

Our tongues tangle together as his hand grips my ass roughly. My fingers are in his hair, holding his face to mine as I kiss him with so much force my lips sting.

"Yes," I murmur into his mouth as his free hand cups my breast, and my body moves toward his palm.

I want him.

Right now.

Right here.

I want Antonio Forte.

The complicated Italian man with an ego that preceded him and gave me pause.

"I need you," I whisper.

He lifts me into the air, placing my bottom flat against the desk. His legs push mine apart as our kiss deepens, and I start unbuttoning his dress shirt.

"Ms. Bradley," Cassie says through the door before knocking lightly.

My eyes fly open as I scramble to break free of his hold. "Oh God. What are we doing?"

Antonio grins and tightens his grip on my leg. "Cassie, we're a little busy. Can you give us five minutes?" he calls out over his shoulder because Cassie thankfully hasn't walked into my office.

"I wish I could, but the board is waiting on Ms. Bradley."

"Fuck," I hiss and push him away gently. "Why now?"

He backs up, watching me.

"I'll be right there!" I yell to Cassie before I slide off the desk and pull my skirt down before trying to smooth out my shirt. "Ugh. I can't go in there like this."

He smiles. "You look perfect."

He reaches for me, but I push him away again. "No. No. There's no time." I groan when I turn to the side and catch my reflection in the mirror. "This isn't going to be our normal office activity, Mr. Forte. I can't go out there like this."

"If I have my way, Ms. Bradley, you'll walk out like this every day. This is only the beginning." He smirks. "Finish your meeting, and then I'm taking you home."

I'm screwed.

I know I am.

How am I ever going to go back to being the hard-nosed, no-nonsense CEO I was before with this beautiful man distracting me at every turn.

I leave Antonio in my office and head into the vulture pit to face the board of Interstellar about the merger.

Chapter 8

Lauren

Antonio hasn't stopped moving around the kitchen since we arrived back at my penthouse. I can't take my eyes off him either. His shirtsleeves are rolled up just below his elbow, tie thrown over the chairback next to me along with his suit jacket, and his hair is out of place as he dices up tomatoes like he went to culinary school.

When the board meeting ended, he barely let me grab my purse before he ushered me out of the Interstellar office and into his waiting Escalade. I didn't fight him either.

I should not have gone into the office this afternoon, and I should have trusted my team to handle everything in regards to the merger. I wasn't ready to face the barrage of questions that I endured for over an hour.

Luckily, Josh stepped up and helped fill in the chunks of information that I didn't have when necessary. I'm still pissed at him for handling the details of the deal without me, but what's done is done.

Antonio glances up for a moment as I gawk at him from across the marble-top island. "So, how did the meeting go?"

"Fine." I lean forward and absently stroke the bit of skin that's not covered near my collar as I watch him wield the knife like he's a Food Network star.

"Fine good or fine bad?"

"What are you making?"

I don't feel like talking about the boardroom or the merger. In fact, I don't really feel like talking much at all, but I know Antonio isn't going to let it go so easily.

He doesn't take his eyes off the cutting board as he pushes aside one diced up tomato and reaches for another. "Pasta sauce. Now answer the question."

"You're making homemade sauce?" My jaw drops. "Doesn't that take hours?"

While on the island, I learned that Antonio liked to cook and he was good at it too, but homemade sauce is an entirely different level of cooking. Something I'd never been able to master in all my years of trying, even though I tried dozens of times.

"Yes, homemade sauce. It's a recipe my mother used to cook when she didn't have a lot of time. Stop deflecting."

I'm chomping at the bit to ask about his mother. He has never mentioned his family before, and I want to know everything about the man I'm falling in love with.

There's still so much I don't know.

I sigh, but I decide to answer the question so I can find out about his family. "Everything went fine. The board had a million questions. Most of which I could answer, and the ones I couldn't, Josh answered without a problem."

A low, deep growl escapes his throat as he tosses the pile of tomatoes in the pan at his side, covering the onions that had started to dance across the bottom. "I'm sure he could."

When he doesn't ask another question, I jump at the chance to get to know more about Antonio. "You haven't spoken about your parents before. Are they still alive?"

He tosses his head back, throwing back the few pieces of hair that have fallen onto his forehead. His hands are covered in tomato juice, and all I can see is the man before me. I don't concentrate on work or the merger. I only see Antonio, the chef with the Italian accent, casual and relaxed. "My father works and travels a lot, and my mother does charity work."

He pauses and stares at me as he wipes his hands clean, but he doesn't give any more details.

"Where are they?" I ask because I won't let him off the hook so easily. He knows about my parents. I've shared so much about my father that Antonio knows more about me than I do about him. I'm about to remedy that and make it an even playing field.

"They live in Italy on Lake Como with my sister and her family."

"You have siblings?"

Jealousy slices through me briefly. Being an only child hasn't been easy. I had Tara, but even then, I wasn't always top priority. Holidays had become something I dreaded as the years passed. All the talk of family get-togethers made my stomach twist into knots with envy.

Antonio tosses in some spices, but I can't read the labels from across the kitchen island. I know it's something he must've bought because I only have the basics. And by that, I mean salt and pepper to season my takeout when I'm home early enough to eat here.

"I have five," he says.

"Five?" I whisper.

"Two brothers and three sisters." He smiles. "You can meet them if you'd like."

Whoa. That's a leap I am not sure I am ready to make so quickly. Meeting family means commitment, and although Antonio has totally captured my attention, I don't know if we've moved to that level yet. "I was just curious. Tell me about them. Are they as driven as you?"

He laughs softly as he stirs the sauce that smells like something from my favorite Italian restaurant. "In their own ways. Enzo, my oldest brother, owns a farm in Italy and produces some of the finest olive oil that you'll ever taste. Catarina, my oldest sister, is an artist. She specializes in restoration work and has brought back to life some of the most important damaged art pieces in history."

"Wow. I wish I were artistic," I grumble.

I was the kid in class who couldn't draw a flower without it looking more like an inkblot test than any actual object.

"Your art can't be contained to a canvas. Your imagination is too big for such a small space."

His compliment warms my insides, and I smile across the kitchen. "Thank you." No one has ever said anything so beautiful about my inability to draw or paint, but his words make sense.

He gives me a quick nod before continuing. "Flavia is the baby of the family and is spending a year traveling the world before she goes to university to study journalism."

"I envy her. I never had the chance to do that, but I wanted to more than anything. Now I don't have time, and I'm too old to go backpacking across Europe."

He laughs, wiping off his hands again and coming to stand at my side. "My dear." He sweeps a few strands of hair behind my shoulder, grazing my neck with his fingers. "You can go anytime you want. Instead of a backpack, we'll take luggage and use my private jet."

His words make my heart skip a beat. "You make it sound easy."

"You're the boss, Lauren. You can do anything you want."

"Leaving the company for an extended period of time wouldn't be wise right now, especially if I did it with you."

"We will have to take some business trips. You're going to need to know everything about Cozza while I learn everything about Interstellar."

I glance down, wishing his words were true. "You're a dreamer."

Antonio places his fingertips under my chin, forcing me to look up at his beautiful, smiling face. "I'm a realist.

There will be a lot of travel in the next few months, and there's no one else I'd rather do it with than you."

"What about your other siblings?" I change the subject because I'm not ready to think about tomorrow, let alone a few weeks or months away.

He cups my chin. "They can come too if they want," he says with a wink.

I playfully slap his arm. "I'm being serious. You didn't finish telling me about your brothers and sisters."

"Let's see." He moves back across the kitchen, putting much-needed distance between us. Although I'd like nothing more than to press my body against his, my stomach is winning the internal battle of wills. "I told you about Flavia, Enzo, and Catarina already. Violetta is a classically trained pianist, and much to the horror of my mother, she joined a punk band two years ago and has been living out of a van as she sings in dive bars. She's the wild one of the group."

I don't know why, but I laugh. "And the last brother?"

Antonio slowly stirs the sauce as it perfumes the air with the most heavenly scent. "Stefano."

My stomach rumbles, but I push aside my hunger pangs when Antonio doesn't continue. "And he's...?"

"He and I are twins."

"I didn't know you had a twin."

"It's one of the reasons I keep such a low profile. I'd hate for people to mix us up because we look so much alike." He smirks because he knows half the time I'm not even sure I like him either. "And Stefano's the nicest person you'll ever meet, but only if he likes you."

"I must meet him because he sounds just like you."

Antonio places the pot of water on the stove to boil before leaning against the counter. "It's complicated."

"You're complicated. How's he any different?"

He gives me that cocky grin that makes my heart skip a beat. "I know, but Stefano doesn't necessarily live his life on the right side of the law."

"So, he's...?" I push my nose sideways with my index finger, giving the signal for crooked.

"What's...?" He repeats the motion with his eyebrows drawn inward.

"Like, he's in the mob?"

"They don't call it that in Italy, but something like that. I don't want to know, so I keep my nose out of his business."

"You're safe, then."

Antonio raises an eyebrow. "Safe?"

"From Stefano stealing me away from you." I laugh so hard, I snort.

Antonio crosses the kitchen with ease, almost as though he's floating as he walks, elegant and smooth. "Baby, I'd never let anyone have you. Not even my brother."

My belly flips, but this time, it isn't from hunger.

Antonio

I still, leaving my cock buried deep inside her. "Say it," I growl in her ear, my front flush against her back.

"I can't."

My finger sweeps across her clit, and her body jolts against me. "You wanna come, baby?" I press my hand

CHELLE BLISS

flat against her, pulling her ass upward and pushing my
dick deeper.

She lifts her head, turning to look me in the eyes.
"You play dirty," she whispers against my lips.

"There's no other way to play." I smirk.

The game had been fun, but now I'm dying for the
orgasm she's holding out of reach for both of us. I may
have given her my position at Cozza, but I'll remain in
charge in the bedroom. The admission is simple for
most people, but the way we started makes everything
more complicated.

"I'm..." She grinds her clit against my palm, trying to
get what she wants without saying what I want to hear.
When I cup my hands, making it impossible for her to get
off, she finally gives in. "I'm yours, Antonio. I'm yours."

Hearing her finally say the words is like music to my
ears. I pull back, arching my body on top of hers before I
slam inside her so hard, her body moves forward across
the bed. She pushes back, meeting each thrust with a cry
of passion.

Every ounce of pent-up energy, frustration, passion,
and longing pour from my soul, building into an orgasm
that could tear us both apart. I slow a bit, playing with
her clit as I pull out and pump my dick back into her.

My spine starts to tingle as the climax grows, radiating
throughout my body. I can't breathe. She follows me,
but not as quietly, as the orgasm grips us both.

"Jesus," she whispers underneath me before I've had
a chance to say a word.

I'm too busy concentrating on each breath as my
heart hammers inside my chest, threatening to break

free. Dear God. The woman does it for me like no one else ever has. I don't know if it's her unwillingness to make anything easy, but every step along the way she's had me by the proverbial balls.

I roll onto my side, pulling her down with me onto the comforter. "Mmm," I mumble, unable to muster any intelligible words.

My thoughts are scattered. Less than a month ago, I had dreams of ripping Interstellar away and making it my own. Now I'm handing the entire company over to the woman I just fucked. Either I'm hopelessly in love with her, or I've officially gone off the deep end.

I close my eyes and stroke the soft skin on her arm as she curls into me. My life, although crazy at times because of business, has never been as peaceful as it is in the moments when Lauren's at my side.

I never thought I'd be here. The last twenty years have been a dizzying array of women parading around and shaking their asses in front of me, hoping I'd drop to one knee and propose marriage. A few tempted me, but none have gotten as close as Lauren Bradley. There's something about her, something in our connection, that makes me want to claim her as my own and put a ring on her finger.

"Are we fooling ourselves?" she asks, peering up at me just as I open my eyes.

"What do you mean?" My post-sex brain haze makes the simplest thought almost impossible.

She raises herself up, placing her hand on my chest as she stares into my eyes. "Can this really work? I mean, we're electric in bed, but..."

"We'll make it work, Lauren." I lift my head, placing a kiss on her forehead and letting my lips linger against her skin. "I won't settle for anything or anyone else."

"When word gets out about us, people are going to hate me," she confesses.

Pulling her on top of me, I brush her hair away from her eyes. Her heart's beating as fast as mine, almost in sync. "Why would they hate you?"

"They're going to say I slept my way to the top."

I laugh softly, touching her chin as my thumb strokes her bottom lip. "You were already at the top, my love. You've proven yourself with the Mercury engine and well before that, in fact. I'm sure every employee will hate both of us equally, but we're not meant to be liked. When you're at the top, the people underneath are forever gunning for your failure."

Tiny lines form across her forehead, and her lips flatten. "That's not always true."

"It's always true. They pray for our failure. It's the only thing they can cling to in hopes of someday taking our jobs. But now we have each other to watch the other's back, so it'll be harder for them to knock us off our game."

Her fingernail grazes the skin on my chest as her features soften. "You really think us working together is going to be a good thing?"

Before I kiss her, I say, "We're going to take over the world, Lauren. We were pretty damn strong separately, but together, we're unstoppable."

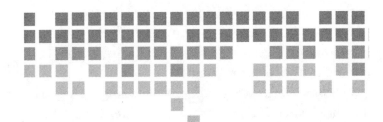

Chapter 9

Lauren

I'm standing in the living room, rubbing my eyes with only Antonio's undershirt covering my naked body. When I woke up, I reached for him, but he was gone and the sheets were cold where he had lain hours earlier.

"Where are you going?" I ask, blinking a few times to make sure the suitcases in my living room are real.

Antonio struts across the living room with a cup of coffee in his hands, and I pray it's for me. "We're going out of town."

I rock backward on my heels in disbelief. "We can't go anywhere."

He thrusts the cup in front of me, and I take it, staring at him over the rim as I take a sip and he speaks. "You can't go into work, and it's almost the weekend. No business will be done for a few days. Josh and Carlino will handle everything in our absence."

I mumble nonsense into the mug as I try to let the caffeine work its magic so I can form a coherent argument about why it's not the right time for us to disappear. Since Antonio's walked into my life, I've spent more time away from the office than I have doing my actual job. Some of it has been his fault, while the rest has been caused by the chaos of Trent.

Antonio backs away, his eyes traveling up my bare legs in a heated gaze. "Everything has already been taken care of. I explained that we're going to spend a few days at the Cozza headquarters in Italy so you can report back to your board about the state of our affairs."

"That bullshit worked?"

"There's a bit of truth to it. I packed your bags, so once you're ready, we're off."

"Off where?" My mind's still hazy and I haven't had enough coffee to fully process everything he just said.

"Italy."

I sway a bit as the realization that I'm going to spend a weekend in Italy with Antonio crashes over me. The country has always been on my bucket list, but I have never found the time to take the trip I'd been planning since college. Although this wouldn't be an extended stay, traveling the countryside and soaking in the culture, it would be on the arm of a man I've quickly fallen in love with.

"Rome?" I'm almost giddy at the thought of the fountains and courtyards steeped in history and sipping an espresso while people watching.

"Como. It's my mother's birthday, and I can't miss it. Sorry to say, I'm going to subject you to the entire Forte family at once."

My mouth falls open as I gawk at him, blinking repeatedly as my mouth closes and opens again. This isn't a casual trip or business at all. He's going to introduce me to his mother and siblings all at once.

I set my coffee down on the table near the couch and rush toward my bags, quickly unzipping the first one. "Oh my God. Did you pack the right things? I can't look a mess when I meet them." I tear through the first layer of clothes, impressed with his choices because it's everything I would've packed myself.

He kneels in front of me, moving my hands away from the carefully and meticulously packed bags. "Trust me a little here. I have everything you need, and whatever is missing, we'll buy. The stores in Como are some of the most spectacular in the world."

Panic slices through me. In relationships, there's always a small amount of lead time for an event like this. At least, I think there is. I haven't had many relationships that have gotten to the point of meeting the parents, but I always assumed I'd have more than a few hours to prepare myself.

"You can't just spring this on me. Oh Jesus."

He smiles softly and places his hands on my shoulders, gently squeezing. "My family will love you. It doesn't matter what you wear, Lauren. They're ecstatic you're coming for the party."

The blood drains from my face at the thought of a room full of people and their eyes all on me. I'm sure

Antonio has brought the flavor of the moment to every family party, and I'll be compared to each beauty before me. "I'm sure they're used to you bringing home a certain kind of woman," I say, drawing in a breath through my nose as I close my eyes and try to calm myself down.

"I've never taken anyone home with me," he says.

My eyes pop open, and the second of calm I'd achieved evaporates. "What?" The panic intensifies because that means I'm the...

I can't even think the words.

"You're the first woman I've ever brought home to meet my family, Lauren," he utters them for me.

I resist the urge to fall backward and curl into the fetal position. Reaching out, I wrap my hand around his forearm and use him as an anchor. "Don't you think we should wait for something this important?"

"I already told my mother, and she's excited to meet you. You wouldn't want me to break her heart, would you?"

I wrinkle my nose and glare at him. "Using guilt isn't nice, Antonio."

"I'll use any means necessary to spend the weekend with you again." He smirks, and his thumb strokes the side of my neck softly as he keeps his hands firmly planted on my shoulders. "But be prepared, there's no guilt like an Italian mother's. She can get you to do anything her heart desires with a single look."

"Great," I mutter and sigh, still clinging to him to stop myself from falling over. "I'll go for your mother and because it's Italy."

"And because you love me."

Those five words are all it takes to cause my grip to slip and for me to tumble backward on my ass in the most ungraceful way. I stare up at the ceiling as Antonio climbs to his feet and stands over me. I seal my eyes shut and block out the world. I'm not ready to make an admission as grand as that. Yesterday, I thought he was stealing my company, and my head hasn't fully embraced the idea that Antonio and I are falling in love with a connection so deep and strong that nothing could tear it apart.

Except for meeting his mother and making a fool of myself. If I don't win her over, we could be finished before we ever really get started.

"I'll be ready in an hour," I say as I roll to my side and push off the floor. "Power up the jet. Italy, here we come." I raise my arm high in the air, giving a little fist pump to no one. Fake excitement is easy when my back is to him because the look on my face is one of absolute horror.

If nothing else, I got out of the situation unscathed and without professing my love for Antonio, even if the words are true. I'm not ready to let go of the one tiny piece I've kept to myself.

■ ■ ■ ■ ■ ■ ■

Antonio whisked me out of the Cozza headquarters so fast I can't even remember what color the walls were in his office. He introduced me to a few people, referring to me as the CEO of Interstellar and nothing more. Most of what he said was in Italian, and I didn't understand a single thing.

I settle into a chair at the café across the street from the modern, almost grotesque, headquarters that don't fit in with the surrounding classical architecture. A handsome man in a crisp white dress shirt with an apron wrapped around his waist approaches and mutters something in Italian.

I smile at him as my face heats, wishing I'd learned Italian in college instead of Spanish. "Espresso, per favore."

He nods, giving me a quick smile before disappearing. Although I spoke the words correctly, the accent I used screamed American, along with the jeans and Cubs T-shirt I'd thrown on this morning before we left the hotel. I thought today would be a relaxing day with us just taking in the sights of Milan, where the Cozza headquarters are located. Antonio failed to mention that we'd be visiting some of my future employees, or else I would've worn something a bit more appropriate.

The waiter sets the cup of espresso down in front of me along with a small carafe of cream and a bowl of sugar. I smile up at him with a quick nod, not risking butchering the beautiful Italian language again.

He leaves me in peace to take in the sights and sounds of the city around me. After I dump two spoonfuls of sugar and a dash of cream into my tiny cup, I sit back and let the realization sink in that I'm in Italy with Antonio.

I think about the thousands of people who have walked down the same street over the centuries or sipped a cup of heavenly espresso in the same seat I currently occupy. Although I love Chicago, compared to a city like Milan, it's new.

"Enjoying yourself?" Antonio says, creating a shadow over the table as he stands in my line of sight.

My gaze travels up the length of him, slowly drinking in the handsome man before me. "I am. Thank you. Coffee?"

He sits down, snapping his fingers, and the waiter comes before his hand has even rested on the table again. The two of them laugh like they're old friends as they speak words that mean nothing to me.

I watch them over the rim of the espresso cup as their hands move around as if they're speaking sign language as well as Italian. Antonio looks relaxed, almost at home for the first time since I met him.

"Lauren, this is Fabrizio. He's been a dear friend for years."

Fabrizio nods and so do I before Antonio reverts back to his native language. Fabrizio's eyes keep coming back to me, his smile growing wider with each passing word. I glance around the street to avoid his gaze.

When Fabrizio walks away, Antonio kicks back in the chair and sighs. "It's good to be home."

I hadn't thought much about the fact that his home isn't in Chicago, let alone the United States. Our lives are on entirely different continents. I'm not willing to drop everything in Chicago and commit to life in Italy on a full-time basis, but in the short time I've been here, I've fallen hopelessly in love with Milan.

"I understand why you've missed it. It's beautiful here."

An automobile flies by, heading down the street faster than any one before, and Antonio's hair blows in the breeze, following the car. "Milan is nothing compared to cities such as Venice. We'll visit them all in time."

In time. I blink. In time. I blink again.

When did my life become jet-setting across the world on private planes on the arm of my handsome, yet sometimes asshole-ish used-to-be rival? I choose to ignore the statement because my brain still can't process the thought of in time, meaning over the years, which terrifies me.

"Finish your coffee, and then we'll head to Como for the rest of the weekend," Antonio says like it's no big deal.

"Okay," I reply, sounding cool as a cucumber.

A boardroom full of hostile stockholders doesn't terrify me as much as the thought of meeting the Forte family.

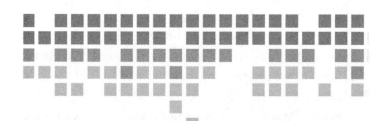

Chapter 10

Antonio

"What if they hate me?" Lauren squeezes my hand as my sister's estate comes into view.

She's been glued to the window since we turned onto Catarina's street. The large estates ranging from old-world Italian to over-the-top modern mansions dot the coastline. My sister's home is no different than the others surrounding the lake with its majesty, reeking of wealth and excess.

"They won't hate you."

"How do you know?"

"My family is the least judgmental group of people."

"Why don't I believe that?" she grumbles.

"I'm an asshole, and they love me."

She laughs softly and finally looks in my direction. "They have to love you. You're family."

I smile and pull her hand toward my lips before kissing the tender skin on the backs of her fingers. "That only means they have to put up with me. I'm sad my father won't be here to meet you. He's away with my brother-in-law, working on a special project."

"It's okay. I understand."

As we pull up to the large iron gates, Lauren snatches her hand away and pulls down the visor above her head. She slips open the mirror, turning her face side to side and making the strangest faces.

"I don't know why I'm so nervous," she says as she sweeps her fingers across her cheek.

The gates open, and we make our way up the cobblestone driveway toward the ivory stucco structure that could easily be mistaken for a resort instead of a home.

"Do not leave my side."

"I won't leave you, but be prepared."

She grabs my arm, holding on to it tightly. "For what?"

"They're a little over-the-top."

"Antonio, it's been years since I've been around a family. I can't breathe. I don't know if I can do this."

I hadn't really considered how meeting my family would affect her. I couldn't imagine having no one left in the world that shared my bloodline. The pain of such a thought is incomprehensible to me.

The entire family is standing outside when we pull up in front of the house. Lauren's grip intensifies as she leans forward, staring at the small crowd of people when we park. "Jesus. That's a lot of people."

"Everyone came to meet you."

She fidgets in her seat, barely able to unlatch the seat belt with her shaking fingers. I reach over, giving her a warm smile as I help her undo it. Before I have a chance to turn the engine off, my mother opens Lauren's door.

"Bella donna," Mamma says, holding her arms out to Lauren and expecting a hug.

Lauren turns to me, looking for help, but there's nothing I can do when it comes to my mother. She's a woman who's used to getting what she wants and has never taken no for an answer.

I climb out, ready to come to Lauren's rescue, but I'm not needed. Lauren steps toward my mother and into her embrace with no hesitation. I just stand there, transfixed by the two most important women in my life meeting each other.

"My girl, you are so frail," Mamma says as her arms wrap around Lauren tightly. "My son has not been feeding you well."

Lauren takes it in stride, laughing softly as my mother starts to grope at her arms, and she slowly backs away.

My mother's eyes rake over Lauren's torso as she holds her hands. "I must feed you. Come."

Lauren glances backward, still laughing with bright pink cheeks. Any remnants of worry and nervousness have vanished within a few seconds of being in my mother's arms.

Catarina wraps her arms around me before giving me a big, wet kiss on the cheek. "We've missed you, but I see why you've been gone so long. She's beautiful."

"She's more than a pretty face, Cat. She's quite simply perfection."

Her eyes widen, and her head jerks backward. "Wait," she says, placing her palm against my forehead. "You don't have a fever."

I swat her arm away and laugh. "I'm fine, just in love."

"You didn't just say what I think you did, did you?" Enzo asks as he approaches with the biggest smile. "Is my brother finally in love?"

They've never seen this side of me. I've always kept the women in my life far enough away from the prying eyes of my family, but I can't do that with Lauren. She means more to me than all of them put together, and I want to show her off and bring her into the fold.

I shrug, unable to hide my smile. "She's the one." I glance toward the staircase leading into the house. Lauren and Mamma are walking hand in hand, deep in conversation.

"Zio Ant! Zio Ant!" my two nieces, Catarina's girls, scream as they run down the stairway, almost knocking Lauren over.

They fling their tiny bodies into my arms just as I kneel low enough so they don't kick me in the balls. "Ah, my girls." I kiss their cheeks and give them a dozen kisses each.

Lauren's watching me with curiosity because she's never seen me as much more than a ruthless businessman. But my family means everything to me. My nieces and nephews have filled the void that had been left when I'd given up on the possibility of someday having my own children.

"Dove sei stato?" Amalia asks while pressing her tiny, warm palm to my cheek and forcing me to look at her.

She's grown in the few weeks I've been away. Every time I see the girls, I can practically see them age before my eyes. I want to keep them small and innocent just like they are now. Wearing their frilly dresses with long curls that bounce in the wind.

"I was with her." I lift my eyes toward Lauren.

She hasn't moved, and my mother hasn't stopped talking. Our eyes lock, and something passes between us. Something that we'd never experienced before. An understanding of sorts, or maybe she finally recognizes the real me that I share with very few people.

"Ooh," Guila, the eldest of the two, coos. "She's pretty."

I don't look away, keeping my gaze fixed on Lauren. "She is."

"Are you going to get married, Zio Ant?"

I laugh and kiss their faces as they wriggle free from my arms to escape the over-the-top loving I typically bestow on them.

"Run, Amalia. He's coming!" Guila screams, running in a circle as I stalk toward them with my arms in the air and make low-pitched growling noises.

"You can't get away." I move faster, chasing them toward the stairway and Lauren.

"Have you ever seen him like this before?" Enzo asks Catarina.

"When he's drunk."

"He's drunk in love, my dear Catarina."

I run up the stairs, giving Lauren a quick kiss on the

lips before I back away, ready to chase after the little princesses.

"I like this side of you, Forte," she says and touches my arm before I slip away.

There's so much of myself I want to share with her. So many things I want to show her, but first, I'm going to make her fall. It's all part of my evil plan to make Lauren mine forever.

Lauren

I can't move. My stomach is about to burst as my zipper digs into my skin. I don't remember a time in my life when I'd been stuffed full of so many tasty dishes at once. Every time I tried to stop, Mrs. Forte would push the plate in front of me again and insist that I had more.

"Mangia," she would say, motioning toward her mouth.

I couldn't say no to her either. She sat at my side, the opposite one of Antonio, and the rest of the family sat with us. I ate while she talked, and thankfully, she didn't ask many questions of me.

Everyone seemed to talk at once, and somehow, they heard each other because the conversation never stopped flowing.

I tried to imagine what it would be like to grow up in a house with so many brothers and sisters. Dinners with my parents before my mother passed away were always quiet affairs in which my parents would ask about school or talk about work.

As adults, Antonio and his siblings are a loud, boisterous group. I can't imagine when they were knee-high and probably barely able to contain their energy long enough to sit for ten minutes.

"How's the takeover going?" Violetta asks from the other side of the table and loud enough that everyone hears the question clear as day.

All motion ceases as every eye in the room turns to Violetta in an icy stare. Based on that, I know his family is fully aware of who I am except for poor Violetta.

Mrs. Forte pops up from her chair. "How about some dessert?"

Everyone ignores her question. The room is so quiet that I can hear my own heartbeat and the birds chirping away in the bushes outside the window.

"I'll take some dessert," I tell Mrs. Forte with a big, fake smile. I can't possibly put another thing in my stomach, but I can't take the silence even more.

"Oh, good. I made it just for you. Antonio said you love tiramisu."

"That's so sweet of him."

Just because I ate two servings, his and mine, at the café in Milan yesterday doesn't mean it's my favorite. But, damn it. That tiramisu may quite possibly have been a tiny slice of heaven. Okay, two huge pieces, if I'm being honest. But after the amount of food I just ate, I can't imagine putting one more thing inside my body and being able to walk out of this room with any type of grace.

Violetta's eyes dart around the table. "Why is everyone looking at me like that?"

CHELLE BLISS

Instead of letting one of them answer, I figure I should field the question so we're not walking on eggshells all weekend. "The takeover has turned into a merger, Violetta."

"Vi, please, Lauren." Violetta brushes her brown hair with purple tips behind her shoulders in a very glamorous fashion.

"Vi." I smile. I like this girl. A lot. She's so opposite of her brother with her wild, carefree exterior, and she completely goes against the grain of the rest of the family. "I guess the rest of the family didn't tell you, but I'm the CEO of Interstellar, the very same company your brother tried to take over."

"Fanculo." She hangs her head and sighs loudly before yelling something else in Italian that I don't understand.

Antonio yells back, his arms flailing about, and within ten seconds, everyone is screaming. Except for his mother because she rushed into the kitchen like she knew a war was coming. She got out of dodge in an instant, and I regret not joining her.

"Basta." Antonio slams his fists on table and glances at me. "I'm so sorry, Lauren."

"It's no big deal." I turn my gaze to his sister sitting quietly at the end of the table. "Vi, please don't feel bad."

"I can't believe no one told me. Please accept my apology."

I laugh softly, grabbing Antonio's hand that's still clenched in a tight ball. "If I can forgive your brother for trying to steal my company, I can get over anything. You weren't being mean. Please, think nothing of it, Vi."

Antonio's about to say something, but before he can, Mrs. Forte enters the room with the biggest tiramisu I've ever seen. "I hope everyone is still hungry."

There's a collective groan as she sets the ornate dish on the table and stands over it. I know I have to have at least a piece because of the way she's staring down at it with so much pride. I've known enough Italians in my life to know food is something you can't turn down without hurting their feelings.

"It looks wonderful," I tell her and place my hand over Antonio's, giving it a light squeeze.

"This is my birthday weekend, and the last thing I want is for you children..." Her voice lingers on the word, driving it home, but I can't tell if she's talking about their behavior or her role in the family. "There's to be no more fighting. Understood?"

"Si, Mamma," Antonio replies along with his brothers and sisters.

"Good." She smiles, placing her hands on her hips as she gazes around the table. "This is a weekend to celebrate, not fight, and we have an honored guest."

My face reddens at the compliment. "Please, don't go out of your way. I'm enjoying every moment of spending time with you and your family."

Mrs. Forte places her tiny hand on my shoulder. "Eat your dessert, and then I'd like to show you around the estate."

I don't know why I was so worried about her. She's been nothing but sweet and exceedingly cordial since the moment we pulled up. I guess I assumed she wasn't going to be open and friendly since her son isn't the most likable person until you get to know him.

But so far, I've become envious of Antonio. Not because of what he's achieved in business, but because he was lucky enough to be born into this family. One with so many people and filled with so much love that he'd never known the loneliness I had in my life.

Chapter 11

Lauren

The grounds of the Forte mansion are beyond breathtaking. The interior of the home is awe-inspiring, but standing amongst the fountains, flowering bushes, and Lake Como, I can't help but fall in love with this majestic country. There's a peace and tranquility that Chicago, my hometown and first love, will never be able to beat.

The words Antonio spoke to me at the W bar come back to me. I took offense when he said Chicago was nice for an American city, but now I understand it. Although I could travel anywhere in the world, I've barely been outside the United States unless I traveled for business. And even then, I didn't take time to soak in the beauty around me. In the last two weeks, Antonio has shown me more of our tiny world, taking me to a private island in the Caribbean and the stunning countryside in Italy.

Mrs. Forte's arm is hooked with mine as we walk along the edge of the lake. The worry I'd felt when we approached the estate quickly vanished as soon as she wrapped me in her warm embrace.

"So, Lauren," she says, and I love how my name rolls off her tongue just like it does from Antonio's. "I heard about what happened last weekend."

I stop walking as flashes of waking up in the darkened room and then the feel of Trent against me wash over me.

She pulls me closer, turning to wrap me in her arms. "Oh, my dear girl. I didn't mean to frighten you with the topic."

I wrap my arms around her, holding on to her tightly. I don't know why, but I break down. Finally, almost a week after my kidnapping, I lose it. Tears flood my eyes, plopping down onto her shoulder, staining her beautiful flowered dress.

She whispers beautiful Italian words in my ears and strokes her hand slowly up and down my back in a steady rhythm. I let the tears come, they fall uncontrollably as she consoles me. She may not be my mother, but she's Antonio's and has shown me more kindness than many. I ache for my mother in this moment. I mourn her death all over again, wishing I could have another second in her arms to help me through this tragic event in my life.

"Let it out," she says, kissing my temple with such tenderness that my tears fall harder and faster.

I don't know why I'm so affected by everything all of a sudden. Whether it's her words or her kindness that finally put me in the space to deal with what's happened without glossing over it.

"Come sit, sweet child," she says softly, guiding me toward a bench only a few feet away.

I wipe away the tears and allow myself one more second of pity before I pull my shit together. The last thing I want his mother to think is that I'm a blubbering emotional mess. That's not me. I've never been that girl, so needy and in need of constant support. That girl died the day my mother was buried.

"Feeling sad does not make you weak."

I drag my eyes to hers, wondering if she can read my mind.

"If you're anything like my Antonio, it's hard for you to show sadness or fear, because you think it makes you weak." She wraps her arm around my shoulder, pulling me into her side before she continues. "But it takes a brave person to survive everything you've been through in your life."

Resting my head on her shoulder, I close my eyes and listen to her words, letting them seep deep into my soul. It's been ages since I've been given motherly advice, and I soak in every word, wishing I could always have this in my life.

Her hand glides up my arm and back down as she leans her head against mine. "Antonio is quite taken with you. I've never heard him talk about anyone the way he speaks of you. It takes a special woman to capture his attention so fully and quickly. He's very much like his father."

"Is he?" I don't know what else to say. Her kindness and comfort isn't something I expected when I accepted her invitation to show me around the grounds.

"My husband was a handsome man when I met him, but so... How do you say it...?" She pauses for a moment before she laughs. "He was so full of himself. I thought he was a jerk and didn't care about anyone. For months, I turned him down, and he'd follow me around like a little dog."

Her choice of words makes me smile. There's a charm to listening to her speak English. "And then what happened? What changed?"

"I was nineteen and walking home late at night after working at a local bakery. We lived in a small village, and I never thought about my safety. Everyone knew everyone where we lived. No one had any secrets, and nothing bad had ever happened. But that night, a man knocked me down and snatched my purse right out of my arms and took off down the street."

I sit up, turning to face her, totally enthralled by this glimpse into her life. "Did he rescue you?"

"Lorenzo came out of nowhere and chased the man down and brought my purse back."

My smile widens. The story seems like a perfectly romantic beginning to a beautiful relationship.

"After he helped me off the ground, he said I had to kiss him if I wanted my purse back. He told me that he was owed such a gesture after he saved me." She laughs a little harder and shakes her head.

"Did you kiss him?" I ask, forgetting all the sadness I had just felt thinking about last weekend.

"I did, and the rest is...how you say...history."

"You kissed him and knew it was love?"

"I'd like to pretend it was that easy, but love never is, my dear. Lorenzo was a looker. All the girls in the village wanted to be his wife, and my parents had already promised my hand in marriage to another son of a family friend."

My eyes widen. "What?"

"Times were different then. It seems so old-fashioned, but my parents never ventured out of the small town and believed in doing what was best for the family to find me a suitable partner."

"But Lorenzo ruined everything."

"My parents didn't like Lorenzo. His family didn't have a good reputation and weren't thought of as upstanding citizens. But after my lips touched his..." Her fingers sweep across her lips as she stares straight ahead as if remembering how he felt against her. "I knew I wanted no one else but him."

"What did you do?"

"We ran away and eloped."

I gasp. "Wow."

"It took years before my parents would speak to me again and even longer before they accepted Lorenzo as my husband."

"What changed their mind?"

"The children. Once I gave birth to our first child, they finally let the illusion of my marriage ending go and accepted us as a married couple."

"You were so brave."

"I was in love and foolish." She pats the top of my hand, turning to me with a small smile.

"Love makes us go against the grain. Even when we know it won't be an easy path, our heart is something we can't deny. I knew when I ran away with Lorenzo that there would be heartache ahead, but the thought of not having him in my life hurt worse than anything else."

"Do you regret it?"

"I did for a second."

"Why?"

"I found out that he set the entire purse theft into motion. It wasn't luck that he was nearby when the man knocked me down and ran away. Lorenzo had found him in the next village and paid him handsomely to steal my purse so he could rescue me."

"Men," I sigh.

"But the man was not supposed to touch me. A year after we married, we ran into the man in the market. He must not have recognized me because he approached us and greeted Lorenzo like they were old friends."

"Uh-oh." I laugh, covering my mouth with my hand.

"Let's just say, it took a long time for me to forgive him. He was very sorry for the lie. But I don't regret a single day I have spent with that man. He and I were meant to be together for eternity. I don't believe that when we die all there is is darkness. There's something more than us, something bigger. Whatever there is, Lorenzo will be with me always."

"You sound like Antonio."

"My son can be quite romantic in his thinking, but rarely does he shower someone with affection and kind words like he does you. He called me last week when you disappeared. I've never heard him such a mess before. He didn't have to tell me he was in love, I could hear it in his voice."

Warmth cascades over me. His mother verifies everything Antonio has said to me before. Everything I know based on his actions, time and time again.

"He saved me," I blurt out.

She stands and holds out her hands to me. "He would've searched the ends of the earth until he found you. Just as I shall search the heavens for my Lorenzo when we close our eyes for the final time. When love is meant to be, we can't allow it to slip away without a fight."

I slide my hands into hers and stand from the bench, looking her straight in the eye. "Yes, Mrs. Forte. We do agree on that."

"And when in doubt, make babies." She laughs as my mouth falls open and my eyes bulge. "Not too fast, but I'm getting old, my dear. You two would make such beautiful and smart children. I'd like to enjoy them for a little while before I go."

"Um, okay." I smile nervously.

Antonio and I haven't even committed to each other, but she already has me birthing her grandkids. Between his charm and the warmth of his family, I can't imagine going back to my life of vodka and work will make me happy.

With the help of his family, Antonio Forte has officially ruined me forever.

Antonio

Stefano strides into the living room as I watch Lauren and Mother talking near the edge of the lake. "I never thought I'd see the day that you'd fall in love, brother."

"Come here, you bastard. I've missed you."

Even though it's been months since I laid eyes on Stefano, it's like not a moment has passed as we greet each other. He's the only person in the family who's so much like me, but it isn't surprising since we're twins. We started life together, sharing the same womb and most things as we grew. When we were younger, we even shared girlfriends when it fit the mood or our tastes.

He slaps my back as he gives me a one-armed hug. "I wouldn't have believed it unless I saw it for myself."

"Lauren's off-limits, Stefano," I say, laying the ground work for the nature of our relationship, along with his when it comes to her. "I won't share her."

His eyes twinkle, and he gets the mischievous smile I'm all too familiar with. "You don't need to say that."

"But I do." And I will over and over again until he understands the severity of my words.

He smiles. "She must be spectacular."

I'd told Lauren I had a twin brother, but I left out the part about us being identical in every way. He's my other half. The same identical genes fill our cells, and besides a few tattoos dotting his skin, our bodies match in every way.

As children, my mother would often confuse the two of us if not given enough time to really study our mannerisms. It was a handy trick we used to our advantage, but since we've become adults, it's not as hard to tell us apart.

"How's business?" he asks as I turn my attention back toward the window overlooking the backyard.

"It couldn't be better."

"I saw Interstellar's new engine on television and wondered how'd you fare with the takeover after such a big media splash and successful test launch."

"Lucky for me, we're merging instead."

Stefano comes to stand next to me. "How is that better?"

"You see her." I motion toward Lauren with my chin before turning to face my brother. "She's the CEO of Interstellar. She wouldn't be here if we were still trying to take over her company. Instead, she agreed to a merger at the behest of her board."

"It's our magical cock." He slaps my shoulder. "It makes the sanest woman beg for a padded room."

I roll my eyes. His statement isn't entirely false because he's referring to a woman I slept with who ended up attempting suicide after I told her there'd be no future. There were no signs that she was suicidal or even had any sort of mental instability. Ever since that day, Stefano believed it was my skills in bed that drove her over the edge. He liked believing it because he figured he had the same skills as I did, but he didn't.

"Lauren is different, Stef."

She's more than a quick fuck. Even when I met her in the Chicago bar, I hated walking out in the morning without saying goodbye. It was something more than a great fuck, and I felt it, but I thought maybe it was the stress of the situation or jet lag. When I found out who she was, I knew it could be more.

"Did you fuck her before she agreed to merge?"

I don't answer right away, waiting for Lauren and Mother to hit the landing outside just below the window before heading toward the bar. "No," I lie because I'm not giving Stefano any more information or ammunition to use against me and our relationship.

Stefano follows and leans against the bartop, watching me as I pour myself a glass of whiskey. He pushes a glass next to mine before I have a chance to put the decanter down.

"Then it must've been your charm." He smirks as I glance up and slide his whiskey in front of him.

"It made good business sense for both our companies."

I'm just about to change the subject and ask Stefano about his business when Lauren and Mother walk into the room. Lauren stands across the room with wide eyes as they sweep between Stefano and me, while Mother heads straight toward Stefano and peppers him with kisses.

"Now, I'm happy. All my kids are home to celebrate," she says, but I can't take my eyes off Lauren.

I should've warned her because it can be shocking to the system, and that wasn't my intention. Part of me had hoped he wouldn't show up this weekend.

"Mamma, come on." Stefano tries to wriggle free from my mother's grip and overexuberant kissing. "Be dignified. We have a guest."

When I glance to my side, Stefano's eyes are locked on Lauren, and I rush to her. I'm not trying to console her, but rather to mark my territory, which is an asshole move, but it's the only thing I can do when Stefano's involved.

"He's..." she whispers, peering over my shoulder. "You."

I place one hand on her shoulder and touch her chin with the other, bringing her eyes to mine. "He may look like me, but I can assure you, we're nothing alike."

"Sure looks like it." She smiles, but she leans forward and kisses my lips.

The simple gesture calms my nerves about her meeting Stefano. I know Lauren thought I was ruthless. But Stefano can come across like Prince Charming, when he's really more like Jack the Ripper. He's the head of one of the most notorious crime families in Italy. It's shocking that he's still alive with half the shit that's happened under his reign. The fact that he hasn't landed in jail just reaffirms that Italian law enforcement is for sale.

"Ah, Lauren." Stefano moves across the room, closing the distance quickly as I'd expected. "I've heard so much about you, but your beauty cannot adequately be expressed in words."

I roll my eyes as Stefano moves me aside to grab Lauren's hand. She blushes as his lips touch her skin, and my blood pressure instantly skyrockets.

"It's nice to meet you," Lauren says with her hand still against his lips.

"It's entirely my pleasure."

I growl at the exchange, ready to pull Lauren away until she shoots me an icy stare. I've never been this territorial about someone before, and I'm not sure I'm entirely comfortable with it either.

I can tell this is going to be a very long weekend.

Chapter 12

Antonio

Lauren's towel-drying her hair, wearing the sexiest silk nightgown that perfectly shows off every curve and the hardness of her nipples. My mouth salivates as her breasts sway with each movement.

"Why didn't you tell me Stefano was your identical twin?" She peers at me through the doorway of the bathroom as I sit on the edge of the bed, transfixed by her beauty.

"I don't know."

I can't explain what it's like to have an identical twin. Most people don't have someone walking around that looks exactly like them, like I do. If I'm being honest, Stefano and I have always competed for the attention of women, especially at first glance.

"You're worried, aren't you?" she asks, setting her towel down on the counter. She walks toward the doorway and leans against the frame with one shoulder, watching me.

"A little," I admit before rising to my feet and walking toward her. "You didn't like me very much when we met. We were enemies. You don't have the history with Stefano like you do with me. What would stop you from deciding that he's worthy of you because the baggage isn't there?"

She wraps her fingers around my shirt collar, pulling me forward. "It's true. I didn't like you."

I sweep my arm behind her and press my body against hers. "But then I did that thing you liked." I waggle my eyebrows, referencing our first night together at the hotel. She laughs softly as I bring my lips within inches of hers. "You remember, don't you?" My cock strains against the fabric of my pants, pressing into her core.

She stares into my eyes, moving her mouth closer as her warm breath sweeps across my lips. "I remember very well, Mr. Forte."

"Want a refresher?" I raise an eyebrow, aching to be inside her.

"Not until you tell me why you think I'd trade you in for your brother."

I tangle my hand in her hair before resting my palm against her neck, feeling the steady beat of her heart against my thumb. "We have a long history together, my brother and I. And you and I have a sordid history that complicated everything."

Her fingers slide under my shirt, splaying against my back as she flattens her body against my front. "But he's not the one who rescued me."

"He's also not the one who tried to steal your company."

"Once the ball got rolling, there was nothing you could do to stop it. But you've done more than enough to make up for it. We're stronger as a team than individual entities."

I smirk against her mouth, wanting to taste her. "Does that go for us as well as our companies?"

She blinks slowly as her cheeks rise into a smile. "It does. Together, we'll be unstoppable."

"Truer words, Ms. Bradley. Now about that refresher…" I let the words drift into her mouth as I press my lips to hers. Soft at first, relishing the delicateness of her in my arms and against my skin.

Lauren Bradley is intoxicating. Never have I been so swept up in someone that I am willing to give up my position in the company and open up my entire world to her too. I can't seem to get enough of her even when I'm buried deep inside her. I always want more.

Sliding my hand down her back, I deepen the kiss, moaning into her mouth as my palms cup her ass. I grind my cock into the soft, silky fabric near her core, and when the friction becomes too much, I lift her into the air and carry her back toward the bed.

She moans as my fingers bite into her skin, and she rubs herself against me. I lean forward, placing her gently on the bed before releasing her. Standing upright, I unbutton my dress shirt while keeping my eyes on her.

CHELLE BLISS

The look in her eyes is filled with longing and want, and it matches my own. Her gaze follows my fingers as I expose my chest and toss the shirt to the floor. Her eyes linger on my pecs, sweeping over my skin as she licks her lips, making it hard not to rip my clothes off and pounce on top of her.

She places her hands above her head and writhes against the bed as I undo the button on my pants. Patience has never been a virtue of mine, and the way the light splinters off her nightgown, showing off every dip and curve, makes it almost impossible.

"Antonio, I need you," she says in a sultry tone.

I strip off my pants, kicking them away from me in a hurry before climbing between her legs. Slowly, I pull down the straps of her nightgown, exposing her plump breasts that are begging for attention. She moans, arching her back as I close my lips around her nipple and flick the hardness with my tongue.

Taking it slow almost to the point of torture, I don't slide my cock into her right away, although the need to do so is almost painful. I take my time, moving between each breast until she's unable to lie still. I'm about to push myself down to bury my face between her legs and feast on her until she's spent and almost unable to breathe, but she grabs my face and forces me to look at her.

"Fuck me, Antonio. I need you inside me."

Unable to wait a second longer, I grab my shaft and rub the tip through her wetness. Her legs widen as her knees fall to the mattress, waiting for me to push inside.

"Say it again," I tell her, teasing her with my cock as I rub it around the entrance to her pussy.

Lauren

I love a good tease as much as the next girl, but right now, the only thing I want is to feel his cock as deep inside me as he can go. I want all of him. Every inch, stroking my insides repeatedly until the need I feel has waned and my body is spent from too many orgasms.

I push aside a few strands of his mahogany hair that have fallen forward, almost covering his eyes, before pulling his face toward mine. "Fuck. Me." I accentuate each word, driving the point home because my patience is slipping.

He pushes inside, inch-by-inch of his cock filling me so deliciously. Even though we've had sex more than a handful of times, each time is more glorious than the last. My body craves him and his touch. I've been drawn to Antonio like a junkie to a drug, but I'll never admit my addiction to anyone but him.

My fingers tangle in the hair at the nape of his neck and I stare into his ice-blue eyes, completely lost in the feel of him. Together, we feed off each other's need. I push against his cock as he pulls out, only to have him slam into my body so forcefully that tingles shoot out from my clit. I'm quickly driven to the edge as each stroke of his cock pushes against my G-spot.

I gasp for air as his body so completely consumes me and I spiral over the edge, digging my fingernails into his skin as I scream out his name. He follows, holding his breath as he places his forehead against mine, riding the wave of ecstasy we so badly needed.

He collapses on top of me, almost crushing me with his weight. I curl into him, pressing my back into the mattress to fill my lungs with air.

"I'm sorry," he says and rolls to his side, finally realizing that I can't breathe.

Laying my head on his shoulder, I close my eyes and concentrate on my breathing and slowing my heart rate. It's pumping so fast and hard that it feels like it's pounding against my chest, trying to break free.

The room is almost silent other than our gasping for air and the beating of our hearts. Tracing the edge of his pecs with my fingernail, I watch the steady rise and fall of his chest with each breath.

I stare down the length of his body and take in his beauty. I knew from the moment he stripped before me that his body was something that could cause women to drop to their knees and worship him, but not until the last week did I realize that the man is so much more complicated and beautiful than his exterior.

I'm falling for Antonio and falling hard. Being here with his family has only amplified every feeling and made it completely undeniable. The love, admiration, and lust that I had before are cemented to my being.

"Antonio," I whisper against his skin.

He moans as his lips find the top of my hair, and his soft palm grazes my arm.

"I love you," I admit with true conviction. I've held the declaration inside, sitting on the tip of my tongue all week, but I never had the guts to say it.

I don't know if it's everything I've been through or maybe it was speaking with his mother, but the words just come out. I mean them too. I've never felt this way about someone so quickly. His love of his family along with his work makes him the complete package.

I don't even think I ever muttered the words when I dated Trent. Something always stopped me from saying it. Maybe my mind knew that my heart was wrong for having any feelings toward him and blocked me. He forced me to say it in the cabin, but I didn't mean a word of it.

Antonio's hand stills against my skin, and he pulls himself into a seated position, taking me with him. I sit next to him with my feet tucked underneath me and wait. He doesn't speak as he gazes at me, but I can read the emotion on his face.

"I love you," I repeat, wondering how I stunned him into silence. He's never quiet and always has some quick reply.

He cups my face in his hands, brushing his thumbs against my cheeks. "I love you too," he says before a giant smile spreads across his face. "I've been waiting to hear you say those words."

"They've been on the tip of my tongue since you rescued me, but I wasn't ready to say them before now."

"What changed?"

I gaze into his blue eyes and feel every bit of apprehension I'd felt about him evaporate. "Being around your family and taking this trip have made me realize there's no one else for me. I said I didn't believe in fate, but everything in the universe is driving us together."

"I can't explain how happy it makes me to hear you say those words. I know it's hard. I've never spoken them to another woman."

My eyes widen as my head jerks back. "Never?"

I don't know why it shocks me, but it does. Since the moment I first met him, I knew he was a playboy. But sleeping with women doesn't involve professing love. Hell, I slept with him too. I'm sure many women have slept with Antonio in hopes they'd be the one he'd fall madly in love with. Sadly, none of them achieved what they'd set out to do. I wasn't even trying, and the man suckered me into falling in love with him.

"Never. It's not a word I toss around easily, Lauren."

"This is so screwed up." I laugh at the insanity of the last few weeks. If someone would have told me three months ago that I'd fall madly in love with Antonio Forte, I would've told them they had a screw loose.

In all honesty, if I hadn't slept with him that night after a few too many martinis, we probably wouldn't be sitting on the bed naked right now. But it's hard to deny the connection and mutual respect we have for each other. What started out as sex has turned into so much more.

I'm verging on tears because of the way he's looking at me. His eyes are filled with so much love and hope that I want to believe that everything will be okay. But there's so much we need to learn about each other in the coming months, and the merger of our companies will inevitably push us to the brink.

"Nothing worthwhile comes without sacrifice. We've been through too much in such a short time for us to screw it up now."

"What are we going to do? We have to face everyone eventually. We're not going to be able to hide our relationship forever."

"For now, we keep it quiet. Once the merger is done and you're sitting at the helm, we'll ease them into it."

I slide my hand up his thigh, letting the coarse hair dotting his leg tickle my palm. "How long until we have to go back?"

"Two days until we have to return to the States."

"Thank you," I say and lean forward, resting my forehead against his. "Thank you for bringing me here and introducing me to your family."

He pulls me down on the bed, settling on his back as I curl into his arm. "I knew they'd love you."

"I adore them. You're a lucky man to have them in your life, Antonio."

"My mother is quite taken with you." His fingertips trace circular patterns across the back of my arms as he speaks. "I hope she wasn't too harsh with you."

"Harsh?" I laugh, making the same drawing on his chest as he does on my arm. "She's a lovely woman. She makes me miss my mother so much."

"Tell me about her, about your mother," he says softly.

"I was so young when she died." I pause and give myself a moment to let the familiar pang of sorrow slice through me before I continue. "My memories of her come in flashes like a high-speed slideshow strung together in chunks."

"I'm sorry."

Nuzzling my face into his chest, I close my eyes and think back to the day she died. It's the most vivid memory I have of her. "The last memory I have of her before she died was the day before my world changed. She took me to the park downtown near the Field Museum. We lay in the grass for hours enjoying the unseasonably warm spring day. I curled into her side, much like I am with you right now."

"Days like that are always the best memories. I don't remember much of what we had when I was a kid, but I remember the times I spent alone with my dad just being together."

"It's so true. I can't remember my favorite doll that was probably sitting on my bed at that age, but I remember the time I spent alone with my parents doing the simple things like just being together in the park. We spent hours underneath the sunshine, and she told me stories about when she was a little girl. My mom was a gifted storyteller and could captivate an entire audience with her ability. She told me stories about the constellations and how they came to be. And she told me that my daddy would be going up there soon to touch the heavens and that we needed to support him. I remember being so torn about him going so far away."

Antonio pulls me closer and rests his lips against my forehead.

"I promised her that day that I'd let my dad go to reach his dreams. She said he'd make us proud and that we had to sacrifice our time with him for the good of science. I didn't really understand everything she was saying to me. I was just happy to be spending time curled in my mother's arms. After that conversation, it's more like flashes for the next few hours between the park and when she put me to bed. She kissed me goodnight and waited at my side until I fell asleep. She was dressed in the most beautiful red dress I'd ever seen because she and my father were going to a gala at the Museum of Science and Industry to benefit the growing space program that evening. The last memory I have of her is her beautiful face as she stared down at me until I couldn't keep my eyes open anymore."

"I'm sorry, Lauren," Antonio whispers.

"It's not your fault. I never saw her again, and more than anything, I wish I'd told her I loved her before she left."

"I'm sure she knew."

"I hope she did. My world ended that night. When I woke up in the morning, I ran into my parents' room, but their bed was empty. My grandmother was waiting downstairs in the kitchen, sobbing. I knew something horrible had happened, but I didn't understand the infiniteness of death."

"We all learn in time. You just learned sooner than most."

"Yeah." I lay my hand against his chest and close my eyes. "With my mother gone, my father and I became a team. He was my world, and I wanted more than anything to make him proud."

"You have."

Before my dad died, he left no words unspoken. There wasn't a day that passed when he didn't tell me he loved me. Not a week went by where he didn't make sure he told me he was the lucky one because I was his daughter. Even though he couldn't follow his dream, he never made me feel guilty because he chose me over his work. Losing someone puts everything into perspective.

The superhero complex most of us have, thinking we're invincible, quickly disappears after we lose someone so close to our heart. Even though I didn't have them in my life for long, I was blessed to have such wonderful, caring parents to bring me into the world.

"Although I wasn't excited about our merger, I think, in the long run, it'll allow us to go even further and do things we haven't even begun to think are possible," I say, knowing I'd have my parents' blessing on Antonio and the new company.

"I have full faith you'll push us into the next century, going further than any human before. Who knows, maybe because of us, humans will step foot on Mars before we die."

"Mercury can make it a reality."

"You can make it possible."

I believe his words. As we fall asleep, I no longer want to walk blindly through my life buried in my work and forgetting to appreciate the wonders of the world around me.

Antonio makes me want more than the corner office with an amazing view. I no longer want to watch others live their lives. I want to do things I hadn't let myself achieve because I hadn't allowed myself to dream bigger.

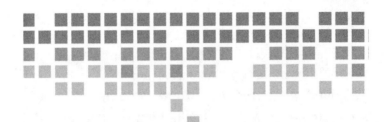

Chapter 13

Antonio

I can barely breathe as Lauren descends the grand staircase in the foyer of my sister's house just before the guests arrive. The black dress I had hand-delivered from Versace this afternoon looks like it was made for her. The silk hugs her body, draping into a pool near her feet. Her hand glides down the railing as she takes the steps slowly and keeps her eyes on me without breaking contact.

"You're one lucky bastard," Stefano says at my side.

"I know," I tell him as she reaches the bottom of the stairs, and I step away from him.

She places her hand in mine and smiles. "This dress is beautiful."

"The dress is only beautiful because of how you wear it."

She can make anything look spectacular. Even when she wears my oversized dress shirts, she could stop traffic with her beauty.

"Would you like a drink?" I ask, ushering her toward the dining room just as the first guests arrive.

"Please." She dips her head in a small curtsy.

"The event is formal, but I most certainly am not. This night is to celebrate my mother, but I assure you there will be more fun than seriousness."

When we enter the dining room, Enzo and Catarina are already standing near the bar, pouring drinks.

"What can I get you two?" Enzo asks.

"Dirty martini for Lauren, and I'll take whatever you're having."

"Whiskey?"

"Works for me."

Catarina walks toward Lauren, eyeing her dress. "God, that dress is a showstopper." She grabs Lauren's arms and helps her spin around. "Gucci?"

"Versace." Lauren laughs, twirling around again like a princess.

"Aren't his dresses divine?"

"The best. Yours is so beautiful too."

Catarina touches the bodice of her pearl-beaded gown and sighs. "It's beautiful, but breathing in it is almost impossible."

"Where are Vi and Flavia?" Stefano asks as he joins us.

"Still getting ready," I tell him as I reach for the glass of whiskey Enzo has poured.

My sisters, all three of them, have always been high-maintenance. Not one of them can get ready in a hurry. They spend hours painting on their faces with gobs of too much makeup and even more time doing their hair. I could never be a woman. So much of their lives are wasted. Lauren is the direct opposite of my sisters. She makes looking beautiful seem effortless.

"Those two are impossible," he mumbles and grabs a glass and the Cognac, pouring himself a glass.

"Will Marcus be here?" Stefano asks Catarina.

"He's away on business. He couldn't get out of it even though he tried."

Marcus, Catarina's husband, is an architect at one of the biggest firms in Italy. He's been working on a project in Dubai for nearly a year, and once it's complete, the building will be the tallest in the world.

Although Marcus wasn't my first choice to be my sister's husband, he's always treated her with kindness and respect. He could've sat on his ass, using her trust fund instead of working to make a name for himself in his line of work.

"Is the project almost done?" Stefano asks.

"What does he do?" Lauren asks quietly at my side as Catarina answers Stefano's question.

"He's an architect."

Violetta and Flavia enter the room, arm in arm and laughing like schoolgirls. Being the youngest children, their behavior was always excused as youth. I miss the days of laughing over the most frivolous things. With age comes complication, but Lauren seems to be changing that quickly.

Flavia clears her throat and tries to regain her composure. "Are you two up to no good?" I ask.

"Angelo just walked in the door and nearly had a heart attack when he saw Vi's dress."

"Angelo is...?" Lauren asks.

"Angelo is my ex-boyfriend," Violetta says as she walks toward the bar, probably needing a drink as much as the rest of us. "Our parents have been lifelong friends."

"Vi broke his heart." Flavia hands Vi a glass before grabbing a bottle of champagne. "He's a pompous ass too. So, don't anyone say poor Angelo."

Vi has never brought home a man who wasn't a pompous ass. Each one is a bigger dick than the last. I fear for my sister's future. She'll never settle down if she doesn't start picking her mates better, but she assures me her main goal in life is fun and not marriage.

With her traveling the world with her band, she's fully immersed herself in the punk-rocker lifestyle. The little girl with the bows in her hair who would sit in front of the piano is gone and has been replaced by a fierce female and bandleader for one of the biggest indie punk bands in Europe.

"Do not sleep with him tonight," Flavia warns Vi with an icy glare. "It wouldn't be nice."

Vi admires her nails and gives Flavia a devilish grin. "Who said anything about sleeping?"

Stefano sets his glass down on the bar and raises his hands in defeat. "I can't listen to this."

"Stop being so old-fashioned, Stefano." Vi slides in front of him before he has a chance to storm out and places her hands on his chest. "If I were a man talking this way about a woman, you'd be perfectly okay with it."

Stefano's eyes narrow as he gazes down at our little sister. I can see the storm raging inside of him as she taunts him.

"Why don't you praise me for my forward-thinking?" She grins.

"You still have the Forte name, Vi. You represent our family and shouldn't be whoring yourself around."

Vi staggers backward. Oh, shit. I don't know if I'm more scared for her or Stefano. Someone isn't getting out of this unscathed.

The shock of his words doesn't last long as she lunges forward and pokes him square in the chest. "Listen, big brother," she says quietly as the storm inside her grows. "At least I don't kill people."

I pull Lauren to my side as I take a few steps away. I've been in the middle of their fights, and typically more than one piece of pottery resting nearby ends up hurtling through the air.

"Did she just say that?" Lauren whispers in my ear, watching them in horror.

Stefano's eyes widen, but he stands his ground. "I have never killed anyone, little sister."

Technically, he's not lying. From everything Stefano has told me, he's never killed someone with his bare hands. Through the years, he has issued orders to his underlings that have led to the deaths of more than a dozen people that I know of, but I'm sure there are even more that I don't know about.

Vi's face scrunches up as she moves closer, getting in Stefano's face. "Maybe you haven't, but your men did."

Gone is the picture-perfect family that Lauren has seen for the last day, and now the ugly side of the Forte family has reared its head.

"You're the one who brings shame upon this family. Almost every day there's an article about some illegal activity with your name somewhere in the text. Who's the one who brings more shame to Papa's name?"

"Don't believe everything you read in the papers. I've broken no laws."

When Vi was younger, she believed his lies. She used to follow him around like a lost puppy, wanting his attention. That was until the kids at school started calling her a killer and left clippings from articles with Stefano's name on her desk.

"Neither have I. And for the record..." She gets closer, more in his face. "If we compare notches, I'm sure yours still beat mine. You're a whore too, Stefano, and a criminal."

Mamma clears her throat, standing in the doorway of the dining room looking nothing less than murderous.

"Oh, shit," Lauren whispers and grabs my hand.

Oh, shit, indeed. It has been a long time since my mother has witnessed a showdown between these two and doing it on her birthday in front of guests is a no-no. There is going to be hell to pay, but for once, I'm not the center of attention.

Lauren

"Let's step out on the veranda. Shall we?" Antonio says, moving toward the guests standing at his mother's side. "Who would like a drink?"

I follow him, clutching his hand as we make our way toward the doors. Passing by Vi, I give her a quick glance. I empathize with the double standard she lives with every day. I don't have to deal with my brothers' ideas of how I should behave, but being in a corporate world that is mostly dominated by men, I'm held to a different standard too.

"Lauren, this is Mrs. Moretti," Antonio says, bowing his head slightly at the older woman. "She's one of my mother's oldest friends."

"It's wonderful to meet you."

"It's nice to see my dear Antonio has found a beautiful woman to be at his side."

"She's more than a pretty face, Simona. She's the head of a very impressive company in America."

Simona purses her lips as her eyes travel up the length of my body, appraising me. "A powerful woman. I wouldn't have picked you to fall in love with beauty and brains, Antonio."

I'm not sure if her comment is a dig or a compliment, but I brush it off and decide she's being nice even if she isn't.

"How's your husband?" Antonio pulls me into his side, probably sensing my agitation.

But I wouldn't do anything to embarrass him or his family after they've shown me so much kindness. I think Vi and Stefano made enough of a spectacle already that his mother deserves a little peace and quiet for the rest of the party anyway.

"He's quite well. He asks about you all the time."

Catarina pulls me away from Antonio and loops her arm with mine. She doesn't say anything until we're near the edge of the veranda overlooking the lake and far away from Simona. "God, that woman is beyond boring and wretched."

"Thanks for the rescue."

"We look out for each other. Even Stefano and Vi. Their relationship has always been tense."

"Always?"

"Always." She turns, looking over her shoulder toward the dining room where finds Vi, Stefano, and their mother.

"I've been meaning to ask you about your English. The entire family speaks it so well. Where did you learn?"

"My parents thought it was important for each of us to learn English. They hired a private tutor to teach us. Every summer from the time we were little, we were only allowed to speak English in the house. When we were told you were coming, we were excited because many of us never get to use it unless we're traveling."

"Whoever taught you did a wonderful job. I wish I knew Italian."

"Stick around this family long enough, and you'll at least learn the bad words."

"I hope this isn't my last trip here. Your home is so lovely, and you've been very gracious to let us stay."

A waiter walks by, and Catarina grabs two glasses of champagne off his tray, setting one down in front of me. I hadn't even noticed that I had polished off my martini and I was carrying around an empty glass.

"Drink it. You're going to need all the liquor you can to get through this evening."

"Is it that bad?" I ask, lifting the champagne to my lips.

She touches my hand, tipping my glass. "Drink faster because my mother's friends are a bunch of stuffy, pretentious women who haven't had a stiff dick in years."

I almost spit the champagne in her face when I start to laugh. Catarina's just like her brother with her quick wit and mannerisms. She has his light blue eyes and the same shade of brown hair, but she is thinner and a good five inches shorter.

"You make them sound horrible."

"My mother is the sweetest woman you'll ever meet, but her friends are old, catty Italians who like to brag about their wealth while snubbing their noses at everyone else. I have the biggest house around the lake, yet they all treat me like I don't belong."

God, they do sound awful. I chug the glass of bubbly wine, polishing it off quickly based on her account.

"Why is your mother friends with these women?"

Catarina shrugs. "They belong to the same philanthropic organization."

"Well, at least they do some good with their lives."

Catarina cackles and holds her stomach. "It's just another way for them to outdo each other. It has nothing to do with helping people except for my mother." Her eyes widen as she looks over my shoulder at the guests piling onto the veranda in hordes. "Puttana."

I've lived in Chicago long enough and eaten in enough restaurants in Little Italy to be able to translate that word without any help. My eyes follow hers, landing on a stunning blond woman in a red dress.

"Who's that?" I ask, unable to take my eyes off her.

"That's Camilla and it's a long story, but isn't mine to tell. I'm going to grab us another drink."

"Okay," I mutter.

Camilla, the puttana in the red dress, gives Antonio a sly smile as she stalks toward him. "Antonio," she says, holding out her hand and continuing to speak in Italian.

Antonio glances down, but he doesn't touch her even though she lets her hand linger in the air between them for an uncomfortable amount of time.

Even though I can't understand what they're saying to each other, I can read his body language perfectly. While she wants him—it's clear by the way she keeps touching his arm—he has done nothing but constantly try to evade her forwardness.

"I'll handle this," Catarina says, handing me two glasses of champagne before striding toward Antonio. The girl has style, and I like her attitude. Catarina isn't afraid of anything or anyone, especially the puttana.

"Camilla, it's so wonderful you could make it," Catarina says as she kisses Camilla on the cheeks. "I didn't think they'd give you a weekend pass for such a small event."

Weekend pass?

Camilla's face drains of color as she pulls away from Catarina. "Is your husband still out of the country on business, or is that what he tells you to get away from you?"

Camilla laughs, and so does Catarina. It's so bizarre, but I can't stop staring at the odd display of friendly hatred being spewed back and forth.

"Want to get out of here?" Antonio asks, and I jump. I had been so transfixed by his sister and Camilla, I hadn't seen him walking toward me.

"Who is that?" I ask as he takes my arm and ushers me down the stairs toward the backyard.

"No one."

I stop walking and give him an "I don't believe you" look as I cross my arms in front of my chest.

He runs his fingers through his soft brown hair and glances down at the ground, kicking at the grass with his perfectly shined black shoes. "Camilla and I had a very brief and fiery past."

He hasn't said anything I didn't already know. It was evident from their behavior that they knew each other intimately. I step away from him, wandering toward the bench that I sat on with his mother near the edge of the water.

"Lauren, wait." He jogs after me, grabbing on to my arm before I reach the bench and stopping me. "I shouldn't have been so vague about Camilla. We dated, but it was only a few times when we were in college."

"We've all dated, Antonio. You seem to be leaving something out."

The caginess in his response leaves me feeling uneasy.

"When I told her that I didn't want to see her anymore, she wouldn't take no for an answer."

"So she stalked you?"

"Not exactly." He glances up toward the sky and sighs. "Camilla tried to commit suicide when I broke up with her. Unbeknownst to me, Stefano decided to pass himself off as me and visited her in the hospital. He led her on and used her. It was all sick and twisted, but that's Stefano."

"Wow. He's a piece of work."

"We were young and foolish, but I've never gotten over the shame of Camilla trying to take her own life after we broke up, and then what Stefano did. When she found out, she came unglued, and her family had her committed to a mental institution for a few years."

I'm horrified and a little shocked by the admission. I don't know who I feel worse for, Antonio or Camilla.

"After she tried to kill herself, I never allowed myself to get close to anyone. I never wanted to be put in that situation again."

I reach out and touch his face, cradling his cheek in my palm. "What she did is not your fault and neither is Stefano's behavior. Did you lead her on?"

"No." He smiles somberly. "But I did nothing when I found out what Stefano had done. I should've stopped his games, but I didn't want to get involved with her again. I let my mother handle it, and it wasn't pretty."

"We all make mistakes, Antonio. As long as you learned something from the experience."

"I don't know if I learned anything useful besides not trusting my brother. What makes it worse is that Camilla ended up pregnant with Stefano's child."

I cover my mouth with my hand and gasp. "What happened?"

"When she found out that it wasn't me, she went into hysterics. She lost the baby and then ended up in the mental ward for longer than she probably should have."

"Again, it wasn't your fault. She knew about Stefano, didn't she?" He nods, but I haven't eased his pain. "I've only been around him for a short while, but I'd never confuse the two of you. Maybe she knew the entire time. Sometimes living with a replacement, especially one that's a dead ringer like Stefano, is easier than being alone and missing the person we love. Maybe she didn't allow herself to believe what she knew was true until the walls came crashing down."

He wraps his arms around my waist, pulling me flush against him. "You're wise beyond your years, Lauren."

"It's easy when I haven't walked in your shoes. I don't know what I would've done in the same circumstances, but it's time to let the past go, along with the regrets that follow you around like a dark cloud."

"Ladies and gentlemen, if you could please join us in the dining room," a voice, which sounds like Stefano, says on the veranda above us.

I sigh and rest my head against his shoulder, wishing we could stay along the shore with the spring breeze of Lake Como licking across our skin.

"Let's sing happy birthday and sneak away afterward. I want to show you something." He grabs my hand, taking bigger strides than I can manage in my high heels on the grass. When I move too slowly, he lifts me into his arms and takes the stairs two at a time.

As soon as his feet touch the veranda, he lowers me down, but he presses my body against his until we're face-to-face. "I want to show you something I've never shared with anyone, not even Stefano."

Now the man's piqued my curiosity. It's my turn to grab his hand and pull him toward the dining room. I've had about as much party as I can take for one evening, and I'll do anything and go anywhere to keep him away from Camilla.

Chapter 14

Antonio

Holding Lauren's hand, I guide her forward on the small, worn path around the lake. "We're almost there."

Even though this is now my sister's house, I grew up right down the street in an equally large estate dotting the coast of Lake Como. The house had ten bedrooms, twelve bathrooms, and could've easily housed a small village. I thought I lived in a castle straight out of the fairy tales my mother used to tell us at bedtime. As I grew older, the house didn't seem as large, especially with five other children and staff roaming the halls.

"Where are we going?"

"To my favorite place as a kid."

Pushing the overgrown tree limbs out of the way, I walk forward and clear the path for Lauren. The moon overhead is full, shimmering off the lake, and it gives us enough light to make the walk possible. When we come to the clearing and the spot where I spent hours dreaming as a child, I turn to Lauren and take the blanket from her hands.

She watches me as I spread the blanket out on top of the flattened rocks that line the shore. "It's beautiful here," she says as her eyes peer across the lake, sweeping over the dim lights of the houses in the distance.

I help her to the blanket so she doesn't lose her balance on the rocks and tumble into the cold lake water, ruining the entire evening. "It's even more beautiful in the daylight."

"I'm sure." She steps onto the blanket and takes my hand before we sit down next to each other. "Why haven't you brought anyone else here?"

"In a house filled with so many people, and with Stefano constantly around me, I used this as my escape for a little peace and quiet. It's the only place I could come to think without being interrupted."

"I imagine that must've been a problem. My entire childhood was filled with solitude, but I can guess it would get annoying sometimes."

I'm saddened by her words. "I didn't mean to sound so…"

"No," she says quickly, squeezing my hand gently. "I wish I had what you did, but I can understand how you must've felt. Your family can be a little overwhelming."

"And loud." I laugh. God, were they loud. We've quieted down over the years, but as teenagers, it was more like a rock concert in the house with all the screaming. I lie back and pull Lauren down with me to look up at the cloudless sky.

"This has always been my place and only my place, but I wanted to share it with you."

She shimmies her body closer and rests her head in the crook of my arm, staring upward. "I like that I know something about you that nobody else does. It makes me feel special."

I roll onto my side, peering down at her beautiful, moon-kissed face as she lies against my arm. "But you are special, Lauren. I've shared bits of myself I've never shown to anyone before. I've said words to you that I've never uttered to another living soul outside my family. I want you to know how very special you are to me."

She lifts her hand, resting it against my cheek. "I know you feel differently about me. I know that I love you as you love me. You're flawed, but I accept you for who you are and who we could be."

"I'm not flawed."

She sweeps her fingers across my skin as she peers up at me with a smile. "We're all flawed, Antonio. It's what makes us human."

Lauren is one of the most magnificent creatures I've ever met. Her life hasn't been easy, losing her mother and then her father early in life with no one else to lean on but herself. I don't know if I could be so optimistic in her shoes. Hell, I'm jaded, and I've had an easy life compared to her.

Unable to resist the pull of her in the quiet darkness, I lean forward and press my lips to hers. My hands slide under her body as I cradle her in my arms and deepen the kiss, needing her more than I need anything else in the world.

When my hand slides up her leg, she grabs my face and pulls away slightly. "Not out here," she says softly.

"But I need you," I admit, inching my fingers higher on her warm, soft thigh.

"What about the party?"

"The only party I care about is here. They won't even know we're gone," I say against her lips before devouring her response with a more demanding kiss because nothing is stopping me or making me leave this rock until I've had my fill of her.

Her fingers curl into my hair as she holds me close and kisses me back deeper and harder. My fingers slide up her skirt, finding the garter belt underneath, and I almost lose it. The vivid picture in my mind of her standing in the light in nothing but her garter belt and sexy matching lingerie makes it impossible to stop and pull back even if I wanted to, but I don't.

Skipping over the garter, my fingertips find the edge of her lace panties and dip underneath. She's wet, ready for my taking. I don't want to rush a single moment. I swallow her moans of pleasure while the pads of my fingers glide over her clit, slowly stroking the very spot that makes her legs fall to the sides as she opens to me.

Lauren

Antonio's fingers dip inside my pussy and my back arches, pushing against the rock, but the pleasure his hands deliver outweigh the painful bite of the hardness underneath me.

"Antonio," I moan against his mouth.

When his thumb finds my clit, drawing slow torturous circles around the most sensitive part of my body, I gasp for air and shudder against his body. My hand curls around his bicep to keep him in place and as a silent plea for him to keep going. His fingers thrust in and pull out repeatedly, driving me precariously closer to the edge and ready to burst with so much pleasure I'm worried I won't be able to stay quiet.

As if on a mission, he drives forward, pumping more of his fingers through my wetness and deep into my core. Unable to wait another minute, I lift my hips in offering. I want everything he has to offer and more.

Antonio's tongue sweeps inside my mouth, capturing my moans as his thumb closes in on my clit. My bottom shifts against the rock, pushing my clit harder against his fingers as my entire body tightens. Colors explode behind my eyelids so vividly it's like a firework display on the Fourth of July. I gasp for air, drowning in the orgasm that's ripping through my system. My moans are swallowed by his lips to keep our location private. My calves ache from the delicious bliss that starts between my legs and emanates to every extremity and fiber of my being.

His lips leave mine first, followed by his fingers slowly slipping out of my body. When I open my eyes, Antonio's staring down at me with nothing but lust in his eyes. He brings his finger to his mouth, slowly licking away my wetness with his tongue, savoring it like it's the best thing he's ever tasted.

"Never anything sweeter than this," he says, closing his eyes as he slides his fingers backward across his tongue and closes his lips around the base.

I thrust myself upright and place my hand on his chest, pushing him back against the rocks. I tear at the buckle of his belt and make quick work of the button and zipper. He lifts his ass off the ground, making it easier for me to slide his dress pants down his legs and exposing his glorious hard cock to the cool night air.

Wrapping my warm palm and fingers around him, I stroke his hardened shaft slowly from root to tip, and he bucks his hips in response. The moonlight dances off his skin, causing shadows across his chest that match my movement.

Leaning forward, I press the tip of my tongue to the head of his swollen cock and lick. He groans and seals his eyes shut, knowing I'm not going to be rushed. I've worshiped his cock before, and unlike some women, I enjoy giving head, especially to Antonio.

I close my lips around the top, circling the crown with my tongue before letting the underside of his shaft slip down. My hands move in unison, working his shaft while I concentrate on hitting every sensitive spot around the tip. He tangles his hands in my hair, pushing my face down and forcing me to take him deeper.

His body convulses as his cock nudges the back of my throat, and I resist the urge to panic as he blocks my airway. Using my free hand, I push his hips back down and tighten my grip around his dick to control the depth. It's not my first rodeo and men always like to push the limits, but I've learned ways to stop them from becoming a little too overeager.

Sucking hard and squeezing tighter, I increase the speed of the strokes, continually flicking the tip of my tongue against the underside of his head. His fingers dive farther into my hair as he moans and shudders against the rock.

"So. Fucking. Good," he mutters with his eyes still closed.

I peer up his body, taking in the way his lips are parted as he tries to breathe and the unsteady rise and fall of his chest as he nears orgasm. Powerful...that's how it makes me feel controlling his pleasure and watching him shatter from my touch.

Spurred on by his desire and the need for his orgasm, I suck harder, faster than I had before. His hips buck wildly, driving his cock into my mouth until my fingers stop his forward movement.

His upper body seizes, and I prepare myself as the orgasm crashes over him. I swallow him down easily because, in all honesty, we've fucked so many times today, I'm surprised he has anything left. Each time I draw back and my lips graze the head of his cock, his body jolts upward as he gasps. Once his arms fall away and his body goes limp, I release my hold and my mouth from his dick.

His eyes open, and he smiles up at me with a small laugh.

"What's so funny?"

"I used to dream about something like this, but I figured it would never become a reality."

I wipe the corners of my lips and suck the tip of my fingers into my mouth before I reply. "It's pretty hard to get a blow job, especially if you come here alone."

"Come here," he says, motioning for me to join him before he stuffs his prick back into his pants and zips himself up.

I lie against him, resting my head near his shoulder, and peer up at the starry night sky. "I wish life were always as easy as this."

"Baby." His hand sweeps up my back, pulling me closer. "I'll always be this easy."

I slap him playfully before leaving my hand against his chest. I sigh, content and happy, as we watch the tiny shining dots move ever so slowly across the darkness.

I want this life. A small part of me has always envied others without such a stressful job. Even after I leave the office, the work follows me home. Heading a major corporation isn't the usual nine-to-five job, rather a constant dance that's interrupted a few hours every day by sleep.

I almost want to run away with Antonio and live on his private island, escaping the world and the companies we helped build. The Mercury engine was my gift, the grand accomplishment of my life, and I don't know if I'll ever be able to top it.

Instead of dwelling on what's waiting for us in Chicago, I look at the stars and watch the beauty as it passes by.

Chapter 15

Antonio

"You missed an amazing party," Enzo says as he sits down at the table across from me.

Lauren and I snuck back into the house just after the last guest left, avoiding any more run-ins with Camilla or any of my mother's stuffy friends. We lay under the stars for hours, watching as the moon crossed the sky, and we talked and almost fell asleep.

I peer up from my phone and watch him pour himself a cup of coffee before he tops off mine. "I'm sure I'll regret the decision to escape for many years."

"Why did Camilla have to come?"

I bury my face in the emails I've ignored for days and scroll through the pages that seem to be endless. "She's always liked the attention."

"It's so embarrassing."

"Good morning," Flavia says, almost skipping into the kitchen in her cutoff jean shorts and tank top that seems to have become her go-to attire. "How are my two favorite brothers this morning?"

"Good," I mutter, switching my phone screen off because there's nothing that can't wait as long as I'm surrounded by my family.

"What has you so happy today?" Enzo stares at her over the rim of his coffee mug, eyeing her suspiciously.

"I'm off to Amsterdam."

I growl. I know the pleasures and excesses the most notorious city in the Netherlands has to offer very intimately. It's like the Vegas of Europe, often a haven for tourists and criminals because of their lax laws when it comes to drugs and prostitution.

"Don't you think you should go somewhere that offers more..." Enzo rubs his forehead, probably experiencing the same dull ache inside his head as me that can only be caused by a sister.

"Culture," I finish his sentence for him.

Flavia places her hands on the table and gawks at us. "I know for a fact each of you has been there. Why can't I go?"

"We're men." Enzo puffs out his chest and puts on the full display. "We can protect ourselves."

Oh God. I cringe and close one eye, bracing myself for whatever may go flying through the air toward Enzo's head. He did not just go there with Flavia. The girl, really a twenty-three-year-old woman, could probably kick both of our asses with one hand tied behind her back.

My mother insisted she take a self-defense class before she turned eighteen.

Enzo and I knew how to throw a punch and even had fancy moves to duck out of the way of a fast flying fist, but neither of us had formal training like Flavia. Enzo never bought into the belief that she could really take down a grown man who was both taller and weighed more than her. But I'd seen it with my own eyes and wasn't about to test the waters.

Instead of throwing a fit and kicking Enzo's ass, Flavia rolls her eyes and gags. "It's amazing you found a woman who would marry you."

Enzo straightens and runs his fingers underneath his chin in her direction. "Don't get me wrong. I know Marquita can kick my ass, but we're talking about you. You're a bag of bones, little girl. You're going to get yourself into trouble in Amsterdam."

"I'm meeting a group of friends there this afternoon. I'll be safe, don't worry."

I don't ask about her friends. Knowing Flavia, she'd lie about them anyway. I just pray there's someone bigger than her who has her back because I have a feeling she's going to find herself partying harder than she expects.

"Just be safe, Flav. Amsterdam can be a dangerous place."

"Yes, Antonio." I get the same eye roll as Enzo received, minus the noise, but I said what I needed to, and the rest is up to her.

I finish the last sip of coffee, wishing I could make this trip with Lauren last longer. "I'll be back in a few weeks. I hope I get to see Marquita next time," I tell

Enzo because she had to stay home with their youngest who was battling a chest cold.

"And you." I turn my attention toward Flavia. "Be a good girl because the last thing I need is jail time."

"We'll leave that up to Stefano." She winks at me before giggling.

I kiss them both goodbye and head toward the bedroom to get Lauren so we can say goodbye to my mother. When I arrive, she's sitting on the bed with my mother next to her, speaking in a hushed tone. They're smiling at each other and laugh a few times as they speak. Lauren looks so relaxed and happy that it's hard to interrupt their moment to whisk her back to the insanity that is our lives.

I knock softly, waiting for their attention before I interrupt. "We have to leave soon."

My mother stands and touches Lauren on the shoulder before leaning forward and kissing her cheeks. "I look forward to seeing you again, my dear girl."

"You, too, Mrs. Forte." Lauren smiles up at her, eyes sparkling in the morning sunlight.

"Mamma, please."

I freeze, shocked at my mother's words because although she's friendly, she didn't welcome Marquita or Marcus to use that word so quickly.

"Mamma," Lauren says, and it rolls off her tongue as she embraces my mother in a quick hug, struggling to let her go.

I understand it. It's always hard for me to say goodbye, but my mother never believed in using guilt to keep us close. She knows I can be here anytime she needs me, no matter where I am in the world. I'd drop everything for her.

My mother glides across the room on her slippers, still in her light pink nightgown that has been her favorite for years. "Be good to this one," she says as she grabs my face. "Don't mess it up." She gives me a stern look, one reminiscent of my childhood.

"Ti amo, Mamma." I kiss her cheeks and wrap my arms around her, taking in the sweet scent of cake and cookies that seems to follow her around. "We'll be back soon."

She stares me right in the eyes before giving me a quick nod and leaving us in peace. When my gaze lands on Lauren, she's wiping tears from her eyes, and I hope I haven't made a terrible mistake.

Lauren

The tears start to flow before she walks out of the room. Antonio's embracing her, whispering that he loves her, and my heart aches for my own parents. For the first time in decades, I felt like part of a family, and it made me long for something I'd missed no matter how hard I tried to block the sorrow from my mind.

When his mother asked me to call her mamma, I almost lost it. Somehow, I was able to keep my composure until she walked out the door.

Antonio rushes to my side, wrapping his arms around me. "Don't cry, mi amore."

I bury my face in his chest, ruining the perfect white dress shirt along with my mascara. "If you break my heart, I'll kick your ass, Antonio." My fingers curl into the material near his shoulders as I take a deep breath and try to regain my composure.

He's laughing at my comment, but I'm dead serious. I've fallen in love with his family quicker than I fell in love with him. Losing him would be horrendous, but losing them would be... I can't even think about it.

I've already let myself revel in the fantasy of Christmas and New Year's surrounded by the Fortes, with their loud voices and flailing arms. Those holidays have always been the hardest for me since my father passed, but this year, I want it to be different. Call me foolish to think so far ahead, but I want the family. I want the Fortes.

He kisses the top of my head, gently peppering my hair with kisses as his hand glides up and down my back in a slow, steady rhythm. "You must love me a lot."

I glare up at him with my makeup streaming down my splotchy face. "I do, but I love your family too. If you leave me, it'll be a blow that could make Camilla seem normal."

Naturally, I'm kidding, poking fun at the crazy ex-girlfriend. I have no room to talk. At least she never abducted him with dreams of a couple's suicide after tying the knot. That would be me.

He smiles, holding my cheeks in his hands. "You've made me a happy man."

My nose scrunches because it wasn't the comment I was expecting at the mention of Camilla. "Because you've made me emotional and crazy?"

"You love my mother and my family, and there's nothing more I could ask for. They love you just as much."

I sit up with his hands still on my face as he gazes into my eyes. "Well, your mother does and Catarina, but the others... I'm not so sure."

"I've known them my entire life. When they don't like someone, they make it known."

"I'm sure," I mumble against his fingers, feeling like my face resembles a guppy fish the way he's holding my cheeks.

He finally releases his hold on my mascara-stained cheeks. "Now, stop worrying. Let's get back to Chicago and get the merger finalized so we're not tied to the city for too long."

I kiss him softly before disappearing into the bathroom to fix my makeup. But as I stare in the mirror and look myself in the eye, I remember something I muttered not that long ago. I said Chicago would always be my home. With Antonio at my side, I don't know if that's even a possibility. His love for my hometown is almost nonexistent, especially the cold, dark winters.

It's a complication I haven't put much thought into since I started traveling the world and falling in love with him. He's made it easy to forget the grittiness of the town I've loved my entire life. But could I make the commitment to him that would forever take me away from the place that held so many memories?

For now, the answer is yes.

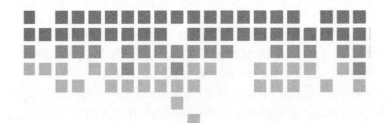

Chapter 16

Lauren

Due diligence, integration planning, executive... All terms that have been thrown around for weeks since Antonio and I returned from Italy. At some point, my eyes started to glaze over after the mention of the words for the dozenth time in an afternoon.

I type a new company email while listening to Josh and three other top executives at Interstellar rattle on about the SEC approval status and how we can't move forward until they've given their go-ahead. In my message, I reassure the employees the merger is moving forward as planned and soon they'll be working for the largest aerospace company in the world, helping us propel humankind further into space than we've dared to travel before.

My email starts to sound like something straight out of Star Trek with its futuristic and tech talk that could rival any Trekkie's vocabulary at the yearly Comic-Con. If nothing else, it's keeping me busy as they hash out the details for a meeting tomorrow with the team from Cozza.

I resist closing the email with a line from Toy Story, a movie I've now memorized thanks to Amalia, Antonio's niece, playing it repeatedly during our last trip to Lake Como. Amalia insisted I sit with her, watching the silly cartoon as she acted out the scenes in front of the large-screen television with me as a captive audience. I hate to admit it, but I loved every minute of the movie and Amalia's reenactment.

"Excuse me, gentlemen," Antonio says before knocking at the door I'd left open, praying someone would interrupt us. "I'm going to steal your boss away from you for a bit."

I cover the computer and mouth, "Thank you."

"No, problem, sir." Josh rises from his chair, flipping his black leather notebook closed. "We were finished anyway."

They file out of the office and dip their head to Antonio. Somehow, they seem more afraid of him than me even though I'm their boss and will continue to be once we merge.

"Ready for dinner?" Antonio asks, striding into my office in the most beautiful gray suit with white pinstripes.

I lick my lips, wanting a taste of him more than any meal. I turn off the computer after I hit send on the email I typed to waste some time and keep up company morale. "Where are we going tonight?"

He grins as he sits down on the edge of my desk and gazes at my shirt. "It's a surprise."

I glance down, realizing I hadn't closed all the buttons on my blouse after our "lunch meeting" earlier today. My cheeks heat at the thought that half the men I was in contact with today probably now know the color of my bra.

"Shit." I fumble with the button, trying to get it closed when Antonio covers my hand with his.

"Don't," he says, leaning forward and taking another peek. "There's no need to button up now. Not where we're going."

I rise to my feet and stand between his legs. "Why, Mr. Forte, are you taking me out for a night of fun?" I blink flirtatiously with a salacious grin.

"Can you handle the excitement?" He brushes the hair that has fallen free from my bun away from my eyes. "You look tired."

"Smooth. That's a way of saying I look horrible."

He shakes his head and grazes my cheek with the pad of his thumb. "No, but I think we need to get away for the weekend and unplug."

That's always his answer to everything. He escapes the city at every turn, whisking me away to the furthest reaches of the planet in a quest to show me all the places I'd deprived myself of visiting because of work.

I close my eyes and move into his touch, narrowly avoiding a yawn. "I'd like to stay closer to home this weekend."

"How about the island? It's a quick flight."

The pull of the waves, sand, and sun, plus knowing that Antonio will be wearing very little clothing, make the decision impossibly easy. "That sounds perfect."

"We'll leave after dinner and make it to the island before midnight."

"But it's Thursday."

He sighs and shakes his head. "One day, I'll get you to take a day off without planning it weeks in advance."

"When the companies are merged and there's no chance of a problem rocking the boat, I'll run away with you anytime."

"I'll believe it when I see it."

He knows I can't take a day off. Every time we go away, I promise we'll have more days like that without such a long time in between, but I always back out when he begs me to run away. Soon, the merger will be complete, and I can breathe a little easier knowing that everything is in place for the new company to run like a well-oiled machine.

That day will come. But for now, we have the island.

Antonio

I'd surprised Lauren and had Tara waiting at her favorite Mexican restaurant just down the street from her penthouse. Lauren says that my family is loud, but Tara gives them a run for their money.

"I kicked his ass out of my car," Tara says loudly and places her margarita on the table in front of her. The green liquid sloshes over the top and lands on the table below, creating a puddle. "I literally kicked his ass." She lifts her leg, plunging it forward, and almost knocks over the waiter standing nearby with the stiletto high heel of her black boot.

Lauren gasps and covers her mouth. "You did not?"

"I don't have time to play games." Tara pulls the salted-rim glass in front of her, causing more liquid to spill out. At this rate, half of it will end up on the table instead of in her mouth.

"Right on, sister." Lauren lifts her glass without spilling an ounce, holding her liquor way better than Tara, which surprises me.

Over the last few weeks, I've spent enough time around Tara to fall in love with her just as much as Lauren is. Not in a sexual way, of course. Instead, she reminds me of Flavia and Violetta contained in one single body. Lord help any man who's able to snag her as a mate. They'll have their hands full for eternity.

"I hope my boot left a mark on his ass cheek." Tara stops talking long enough to take a sip, and I use the opportunity to do something I don't often do, be gracious and selfless.

"Tara, how would you like to come to the island with us for the weekend?"

In an almost robotic motion, Lauren turns to me with wide eyes, her mouth opening and closing like a fish out of water. Tara's face matches Lauren's because I'm sure they've had more than one girl talk about my asshole tendencies and the way I've been monopolizing Lauren's time.

Tara's glass lands a little harder on the table this time, more liquid spilling over the side. "You'd do that?" She slams her hands down next to her glass and turns her head sideways, putting her ear closer to hear me better. "You shittin' me, Forte?"

"Sweetheart, are you sick?" Lauren places the palm of her hand on my forehead as her eyebrows draw together and she moves closer.

I pull her hand away and laugh. "I figured we could have some fun in the sun, and you two deserve a little time together too. I'm sorry I've kept her from you so often. I know how important you are to each other."

"Well, fuck." Tara snatches her phone off the table, which had somehow missed the waterfall of tequila falling nearby, and she stabs at the screen a few times.

"Tara has to work this weekend. You know those are her busy days."

Tara glances up, giving Lauren the evil eye. "Shut your whore mouth. I'm not missing a free trip to the Bahamas. My job can kiss my ass just like that fool I kicked out of my car. Forte, I accept your invitation, but I require a hot pool boy for me."

"Sorry, Tara. There's only going to be the three of us on the island."

She pouts for a second but quickly rebounds. "Unlimited bar and food?"

"That I can do."

She almost hurls herself across the tiny bar table in my direction. "You're the best boyfriend Lauren's ever had."

"It's not hard to top the last," I say with a laugh.

"I'll have my bags packed and meet you at the office at five?"

"I'll have a car pick you up to bring you to us at the airport."

She taps her chin and tries to remain calm, but I can see she's about to burst at the seams. "How many checked bags do I get?"

"It's a private plane, silly. There's no limit."

I can see it now. Tara's going to pack like she's going on a worldwide tour and won't return for at least six months.

Lauren must be thinking the same thing because she says, "Just remember, it's an island. We're not going out. I barely wear anything at all when I'm there."

"What about you, big boy?"

I glance at Lauren, letting her field that one. The last trip we took, I barely kept my clothes on because there's something so freeing about nudity on a private island. If someone came by on a kayak or their yacht, it wasn't my problem if they saw more than they bargained for.

"We both wear swimsuits, Tara, but not much else. Just bring your suit and sunscreen. It can all fit in that giant purse of yours."

Tara flings her black-and-white striped purse that's as big as most carry-on luggage into her lap. "But my makeup."

Lauren rolls her eyes and gives in. "Fine, bring whatever you want."

"Smart," I mutter because I've learned just to give in when it comes to the whims of women. Not many of them could travel with only a swimsuit and nothing else.

"Ugh. I have to go," Tara says, glancing down at her phone as the screen lights up.

"It better not be him," Lauren warns her.

"Who?"

"The ass guy."

Tara groans. "It's not. It's work. They want me to cover the late shift and close down the bar since I have a family emergency this weekend. I should've waited until tomorrow to call off this weekend."

"You can sleep on the plane tomorrow. It has a private bedroom." Lauren smiles and grabs my hand. "Antonio travels in style."

"I'm sure he does, and I'm sure it's come in handy more than once."

I laugh uncomfortably and squeeze Lauren's hand. Sure, a few women have been in that bed with me, but not since the day Lauren smashed into my world and turned everything on its head.

Tara kisses us goodbye and runs out of the restaurant to hail a cab.

"Can she work like that?"

"She works at a bar. She'll be fine. And she only had two drinks."

"Let's call it one since most of the last glass is on the table."

Lauren laughs and wraps her arms around my neck. "I don't know what got into you, but thank you." She rubs her nose against mine and stares into my eyes.

"You could use a little fun with your friend. We'll have plenty of time for the two of us."

"Shit." Lauren rests her head against my forehead and sighs. "Where is she going to sleep?"

"She can use the guesthouse so she doesn't have to see or hear us."

"Thank God. I would've hated to call her and tell her we changed our mind."

"We could've kept our hands off each other for the weekend if we had to, Lauren."

I'm lying, of course. Since we've known each other, keeping our hands to ourselves hasn't been our strong suit.

She lifts her head and fans her face with her hand. "You may be able to, but you've never seen yourself when the water cascades down your body, pooling in the ridges of your muscles."

"You've never seen the way the light bounces off the water droplets on the swell of your breasts, so we're even."

"Let's go to my place," she says.

I've started staying at Lauren's place more often than going back to the hotel where we met, even though it's just down the street. It's become harder to spend time away from each other too. Our days are filled with business, but I always have her nights.

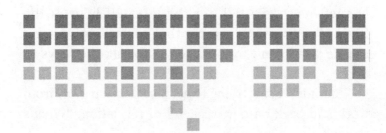

Chapter 17

Lauren

The sun hung above the horizon as the plane touched down on Nassau, the closest major island to Antonio's estate. Tara squealed like a little kid as we flew over the aquamarine water of the Caribbean.

"Shut the front door," she exclaims. "I can see the bottom."

I've taken the beauty below us for granted every time we've made the flight since the first time he brought me here. My attention was always on Antonio or talking with him about work. I hadn't really taken the time to appreciate the majesty and perfection as we flew overhead.

"It's stunning, isn't it?" I ask her as I glance out her window, staring down at the same patch of sand.

"It's the most beautiful thing I've ever seen," she whispers.

Antonio's been pecking away at his phone and has left us to girl talk for the last half hour of the flight. I'm starting to worry that something's wrong but he just hasn't found a way to break the news to me.

"Antonio," I say, trying to get his attention away from work and back on our weekend of relaxation. "What's wrong?"

He sets the phone down on the chair next to him and leans his head back. "It's Stefano."

"Is he hurt?" Naturally, I jump to conclusions because the man's dangerous, and it's not out of the realm of possibility.

"Worse."

I gasp, almost hurling myself across the plane and into his lap. "Oh my God." I grab his face, wanting to shower him with love and take away his pain.

"No. No," he says, grabbing my shoulders to stop my assault. "He's fine, but somehow he heard about our weekend at the island and he was nearby, so he's waiting there for us."

"Stefano?" Tara turns and raises an eyebrow.

"But this is our weekend," I whisper in his ear, throwing off death rays with my eyes. "He's going to ruin everything."

"Hello," Tara calls out because neither of us has answered her. "Clue a girl in."

Antonio looks over my shoulder as I sit in his lap and try not to go ballistic. "He's my brother."

"He's his very dangerous brother."

Stefano, while being made of the same genes as Antonio, is not the same in any other way. I like the man, but sometimes he leaves a sour taste in my mouth. I don't know if it's his illegal activities or his blasé attitude when it comes to women, but I pray he finds someone to put him in his place.

"Is he single?"

All the blood drains from my face. Tara has done some crazy-reckless shit in her life, but inviting Stefano into her world is something I couldn't stomach. "You are not going to date Antonio's brother."

She smirks. "Who said anything about dating?"

Antonio turns me in his lap like a rag doll and wraps his arms around my waist. "I have to agree with Lauren on this one, Tara. Stefano isn't like any other man you've ever met. He's too dangerous to play around with."

Tara goes back to staring out the window as we approach the airport in Nassau. "You two seriously need to calm down. We're on vacation with nothing but sun and sand. What could go wrong?"

***

Stefano's waiting for us on the beach as our boat pulls up to the dock. He's shirtless, tanned, and wearing the most ridiculous hat I've ever seen, but somehow, he makes it look good.

Tara turns to Antonio with her eyes wide. "He's your identical twin?"

"Yeah." Antonio gives her a nervous smile.

"Like, how identical?" She glances down at his crotch, and I can't help but lose it.

"Pretty much the same." Antonio gives me the side-eye, and I sober quickly.

Maybe this wasn't the best idea. I shouldn't be laughing. It's kind of strange to think that he's packing the same dick as Antonio. I hadn't thought about Stefano in that way, not even in the least. I should've known though, but it never crossed my mind.

"This could be fun." Tara rubs her hands together as Antonio tethers the boat to the dock so we don't lose our ride home.

Stefano waves in our direction and flashes a beautiful white smile that nearly glows against his dark skin. If I didn't know the man, I'd think he was almost friendly.

"Hey," he says, running up to the boat and grabbing the handle of Tara's bag just as she lifts it in the air. "Let me help you."

"Thanks." She blushes and lets him take it from her hands.

Packing light isn't in her vocabulary. Even after we explained to her that she didn't need to bring many clothes, I swear to God she packed her entire closet inside the oversized suitcase.

I resist the urge to roll my eyes or make any noise that might start the weekend off on a sour note. Stefano is Antonio's brother, and even with all of his bullshit, they love each other. Because of that, I'll set my feelings for Stefano aside and try to get to know him better.

"Love the ink," Tara says as she walks next to Stefano up the beach.

MERGER - TAKEOVER DUET #2

She's always been a sucker for the tattoos and bad boys. Stefano is like the holy grail of bad decisions and right up her alley.

"We're fucked, you know," I tell Antonio quietly as they walk ahead of us.

"They're adults. They'll never work anyway, but let them have a little fun and they never have to see each other again."

I sigh and stomp my feet as we walk toward the main house.

"You can share the guesthouse with me," Tara offers, and my angst goes from simmering to ballistic. Stefano whispers something in her ear, and she giggles all dainty and un-Tara-like.

I hadn't even thought about the sleeping arrangements, but I should've. I knew there wasn't room for another person in the main house. Well, there is room, but there are no walls, which could lead to a very uncomfortable situation.

"Hey, guys." Stefano turns, walking backward at Tara's side. "We're going to get settled in and unpack. Meet you on the beach in an hour for drinks?"

Tara fist-pumps the air as she dances across the sand. "I like the way this man thinks."

At least two of us are happy.

Antonio

"He's not that bad." I don't know if I'm trying to convince her or myself that my brother isn't the asshole I've made him out to be. Hell, he's done a good enough job sending that signal loud and clear without my help. But from what I know about Tara, she isn't the type of girl who would need rescuing from a man like my brother.

Although he's dangerous, I've never seen him put his hands on a woman. Never. And I've seen some pretty crazy shit happen, from a simple slap from a clubgoer to a full-on knee to the balls. Stefano never struck back because he knew my mother would kill him. In her mind, anything short of attempted murder wasn't a reason to touch a woman.

Lauren pulls a flowery sundress over her head and levels me with her gaze. "Just make sure this is a one-time deal."

"I don't see either of them settling down anytime soon, do you?"

She groans as she pulls her hair up into a messy ponytail. "I'm not taking any chances. We weren't looking to settle down when this—" she waves her arms between us "—happened."

She has a point. A very valid point. I wrap my arms around her waist and pull her against me. "You thought I was an asshole when you found out who I was, and you were wrong."

"So," she says, placing her hands on my shoulders with a serious look. "You're saying your brother isn't an asshole?"

"Oh, he is, but everyone finds the asshole part of him eventually."

"You're insane." She leans forward, kissing my lips as I slip my hands underneath her dress and grope her ass.

"Let's stay in here and leave them on the beach."

She backs away and glares at me. "Absolutely not. We are not leaving them outside alone."

I'll add this to the list of times my brother has stopped me from getting laid, and this time, we're not kids. "If it'll make you happy."

Her fingers wrap around my shirt and pull me upward. "We have a girl to protect." She points toward the sand, and my eyes follow her finger.

In the distance, Stefano and Tara are sitting on a blanket near the edge of the water, sipping champagne and bathed in the light of tiki torches he must've dug out of storage. They're cozy and sitting close to each other as they stare into the darkness.

Lauren is still pointing, and the tiny lines around her mouth that only appear when she's mad are well-defined. "That cannot happen."

"Let's go outside so you don't lash out at me and we end up in bed, making mad, passionate love all night."

She looks at me almost cross-eyed because she's mad and my comment didn't amuse her. "Grab another bottle of wine. This is going to be a long night."

I grabbed two I already had chilling in the wine fridge that the staff had filled before Stefano arrived, along with two glasses. The guesthouse had been fully stocked too, so Tara didn't go without and feel like she was bothering us by having to come to the main house.

"Oh, hey," Tara says, glancing up from the blanket where she and Stefano are sitting a little too close for Lauren's comfort. "Your brother was just telling me some great stories about your family."

I don't even ask because knowing Stefano, it's something that makes him look like a saint while the rest of the family is about to burst into flames for their sinful acts.

"Sit. Sit." Stefano grabs the wine from my hands and makes quick work of opening it.

As we sit, I stare at Lauren, Lauren stares at Tara, and Tara's making goo-goo eyes at Stefano. It's time to defuse the situation and switch to something lighter and less stressful for the entire group.

"How did the tables treat you?" I ask Stefano because, much like myself, the man has a love of gambling.

"I was up until yesterday. But this morning, I lost fifty grand on blackjack."

Tara spits out her wine, thankfully making it back into the glass instead of soaking us all. "Fifty thousand pennies?" she asks, wrinkling her nose.

"No, darling." Stefano lays on his accent heavier than normal because he knows how American women find it sexy and irresistible. "Dollars." He laughs softly as he fills our glasses.

Her face drains of blood, and she gives him the side eye. "Do you know what you could've done with that much money?"

"Tara," Lauren says and shakes her head.

"What?" Tara shrugs. "I'm just saying, fifty thousand dollars could fill my closet with the most spectacular high heels."

"I could still fill your closet many times over." Stefano lifts Tara's hand to his lips in a suave move.

"You're not filling her anything," Lauren grits out, and I almost choke on my wine.

"Lauren, my love, I sense some hostility."

I glance toward the sky and wait for Lauren to explode in a glorious display of feminine anger.

"I'm sorry, Stefano. I'm being rude." She digs her fingers into the corners of her eyes and takes a deep breath. "Tara is my best friend, and I don't want you leading her on."

Stefano smiles and turns toward Tara. "Who said I'm leading her on? Your friend is quite striking."

Tara waves Lauren off. "Loosen up, Lauren. We're just having some fun. Live a little and stop taking everything so damn seriously."

"Can I talk to you in private?" Lauren motions to the side with her head.

Tara climbs to her feet without a word and heads far enough away from the blanket not to be overheard. Lauren follows with her arms down at her sides like a woman possessed.

"I'm sorry if I ruined the weekend." Stefano swirls the wine around in his glass, watching the liquid as it moves. "I'm just enjoying myself, and so is Tara."

"Do not mess up my relationship by playing with her best friend's head," I warn him with an icy stare.

"Give me a little credit, will you?"

I probably should be warning him about Tara because if anyone can "handle" Stefano, it's her. Based on everything Lauren has told me, Tara could make it up the ranks of Stefano's organization with her attitude and nearly deadly stilettos.

I glance toward the ladies, who are speaking very quietly, but their hands are waving wildly in the air.

Tara's not taking an ounce of Lauren's shit, laying into her. Lauren kicks at the sand near her feet and looks guilty.

"I'm going to give you this one chance to redeem yourself. If you ever want to be a part of my life going forward, you'll do the right thing."

"I'm a man of honor."

I laugh and shake my head because honor never enters into his vocabulary when it comes to pussy. Stefano is ruthless in his pursuit of women and the pleasures of the flesh.

Tara hugs Lauren, whispering in her ear, and Lauren laughs. Whatever they said to each other, I hope the mood turns lighter. The last thing I want is for it to ruin our weekend that was supposed to be relaxing.

"All better?" Stefano asks as Tara steps onto the blanket.

He holds out his hand, helping her down, and she bats her eyelashes, not seeming to be fazed by anything she and Lauren said to each other. "We're good. Just needed a heart-to-heart."

I look at Lauren as she sits down next to me. She gives me a genuine smile, and I hope we've turned a corner or else I'll be shipping Stefano off to the mainland tomorrow.

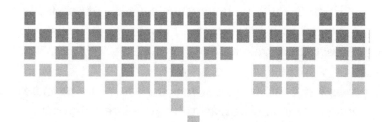

Chapter 18

Lauren

Antonio hasn't let me out of bed since my eyes opened. Not even to pour myself a cup of much-needed coffee. He pulled me back into his arms and mumbled the word relaxation before he drifted back to sleep.

I've been staring at the coffeepot for over an hour, listening to Stefano and Tara laughing on the wraparound deck while I am trapped underneath Antonio's weight.

I try to wriggle free, but it's no use. Antonio's too heavy.

"Don't go," he groans and pulls me tighter against his body.

"Coffee." It's the only word I can muster, not able to form complete sentences without caffeine in my system.

His palm sweeps over my breast and sends shock waves through my system. I can't believe my body isn't numb after the night we had, from both drinking too much and the sexathon after we returned to the main house, leaving Stefano and Tara on the beach.

"I have something better than coffee." He grinds his hard cock against my leg, and I close my eyes, relishing the feel of him against me.

I try to push him away as the dull pain between my legs intensifies, increasing in severity at the mere thought of one more orgasm. "I'm too sore right now."

He props himself up next to me and slings his arm back across my chest. "Are you going to be able to relax today with them here?" His head dips toward the patio where they're still laughing.

"Yeah." I smile up at him.

When Tara pulled me to the side, she read me the riot act. She reminded me about Vinny, a man she dated last year who wasn't on the up-and-up. After Tara fell head over heels for the bastard, she almost got herself killed leaving a club on his arm. One of his enemies decided to empty the clip of his gun inside both of them, but he somehow missed after being tackled to the ground by Vinny's security. After that, Tara ended things with him, but not before she caused a little bloodshed of her own and told him to lose her number.

Tara's probably the strongest person I know. Any one of Beyoncé's songs could be about Tara and her fierceness. She puts up with no one and nothing, taking no shit from the people she chooses to have in her life. It's the only reason I can stomach her hanging around with Stefano this weekend. She assured me that even if she does have sex with him, the things that happen on this island will stay on this island. She said it was like Vegas and I needed to calm down and treat her like an adult instead of my child.

She's right.

It isn't my job to protect her, and I probably should be protecting Stefano from her because he doesn't understand how deadly her right hook is or her high heel.

"I think the weekend will be good for both of them," I say because how could it be any worse.

They're both consenting adults. Stefano is a manwhore, but Tara isn't Mother Teresa either. The woman could probably go notch for notch with Stefano Forte.

"Good." Antonio grins and finally frees me from his weight. "Let's grab a cup and check out the weather. I think we need to take the jet skis out."

I fling myself out of the bed like a pole vaulter and run to the coffeepot, forgetting that I'm not dressed. Halfway across the living room, I freeze and cover my breasts with one hand and my pussy with the other. Way to go, genius. The thought of both coffee and jet skis made me lose my mind and forget the fact that I had a captive audience only feet away.

"Good morning," Stefano says, turning around as I dance from one side to the other.

"Shit," I mumble.

Tara's laughing, almost hysterical at the fact that I'm naked as the day I was born. I'm dying a little inside because their eyes are on me. While she's the one to show off her skin, basically her breasts because they're great and she could give two shits what anyone thinks, I've always been the buttoned-up one who barely flashes my collarbone in public.

"Turn around," I screech and back up, knowing I can't turn around or I'll show them my very white, sunless ass. "Do it now."

Tara and Stefano glance at each other and laugh before facing across the sand to the ocean. When I turn, Antonio's laughing softly and wrapping the sheet around his waist so he doesn't suffer the same fate.

"You could've warned me," I tell him as he walks toward me with enough of the sheet hanging out that I can cover myself too.

"You took off so fast, I didn't get a chance."

"Well, it's coffee." I don't need to say anything else. It's my lifeblood, and I can't really form a coherent thought until I've had at least a cup. That is even more evident after my little nudie show this morning.

I hide behind the sheet and reach for my bathing suit, figuring I can skip a dress today. The suit covers way more than my hand does, so everyone's already seen what I have to offer. Plus, we're going to hit the water as soon as I have enough coffee in my system that I don't end up killing myself or Antonio. After I get dressed and make a beeline for the coffeepot, Antonio wanders into the bathroom and leaves me alone with Tara and Stefano.

"Sleep well?" I ask as I step onto the deck and take a giant whiff of the piping hot coffee that smells like magic in a mug.

"I haven't slept that well in ages." Tara blushes, peering at Stefano under her eyelashes.

"Tara snores," Stefano adds. "Very loudly."

I take the seat next to Tara and pull my knees up to my chest as I grip the coffee mug like it's the most precious thing in the world. "I'm well acquainted with Tara's sleeping while everyone else is awake."

Stefano waves his hand and winks at Tara. "I don't sleep very much anyway. The bed was a little slice of heaven."

"Oh, I know. Wasn't it divine?"

That answers that question. I sip my coffee and try not to think about the fact that Stefano and Tara are not only sharing a bed, but probably ended their night much the same way Antonio and I did.

"Morning," Antonio says as he makes a grand entrance, wearing nothing but his swimming trunks and a smile.

"It's still so weird that there's two of you." Tara's eyes move to Antonio and back to Stefano. "I don't think I'd like someone walking around wearing my face."

"I don't know any other way," Stefano tells her and grabs their two coffee cups from the table that's between them. "More?"

"Please." Tara bats her eyelashes and is laying it on mighty thick.

"I'll go get the jet skis ready." Antonio kisses my cheek. "I know a little ride around the ocean will help wake you up."

I turn my head and kiss his lips before he walks away. Tara's gawking at me as we sit alone on the deck, and I

CHELLE BLISS

can feel it even though I'm not looking at her. "What?" I ask, staring into my coffee mug and avoiding turning in her direction.

"You're a lucky girl."

"What?" I can't help but face her now. "What on God's green earth are you talking about?"

"They're identical in every way, right?"

"Yeah."

Tara waggles her eyebrows and smiles so wide I can see every tooth in her mouth.

"Don't say it."

"He's packing quite the package."

"Ugh," I groan and close my eyes. "I didn't want to know if you'd slept with Stefano."

"I'm proud of you," she says.

"For what?" I grumble against the rim of the cup before taking a giant gulp because I will need a refill before we hit the water.

"For getting the guy with the biggest pecker I've ever seen and keeping him."

I roll my eyes. "Thanks," I tell her just as Stefano walks back onto the deck.

I use his entrance as my cue to head into the house and down another cup of coffee. Besides it being weird that another man walks around with the same face as my boyfriend, it's even weirder that my best friend now knows exactly what he's working with.

Antonio

I collapse on the shore, covered in sand as I shield my eyes from the sun. "Those girls play hard."

184

After two hours on the jet ski, I needed a break, and my brother followed me in. Tara and Lauren decided to stay out on the water to give us a little brother time together.

Stefano sits at my side, watching Tara and Lauren speed through the water, jumping waves and screaming loudly. "They're quite a pair."

"What are you doing here?"

My brother doesn't vacation and hasn't joined me for a trip in years. When he called, to say I was surprised would be an understatement. But now he's getting comfortable with Tara, and I'm wondering if I made a huge mistake by letting him join us.

"I needed to get away for a few days."

"Authorities after you?"

It's a logical question given his line of work, and I hate that my brother didn't choose a path like mine. He could've headed a major corporation without a problem. The man has balls of steel as well as a mind that never turns off.

"No one is after me. I just needed to get away from it all. The life is wearing on me."

"Most people in your line of work don't live long enough for anything to wear on them."

He lies back and spreads his arms wide. "I think it's time for me to make a change before I end up six feet underground in an unmarked grave."

I sit up, surprised by his statement. "You're really going to quit?"

Stefano has always defended his lifestyle. But no matter how he tried to spin it, I knew exactly what he did. Movies like The Godfather tried to romanticize the Italian Mafia, especially for people outside of Italy, but it wasn't as pretty or as sexy as the movie studio portrayed.

"I think it's time to join the ranks of law-abiding citizens."

"Do they just let you out?"

I know it doesn't work that way. Not even in the movies does someone just hang up their hat and walk off into the sunset. Stefano knows enough that he could bring down the entire organization.

"No, but I found a way to make it happen."

"What are you going to do?"

"Nothing. I have enough money to never work again."

I lie back down, close my eyes, and smile. "I can't imagine you doing nothing, but it's better than what you've been doing your entire life."

"I'll find ways to entertain myself." He laughs softly.

I turn my head, blocking my eyes from the sun overhead. "And Tara?"

He looks at me, and I almost see a glimmer of humanity in his expression. "She's fun. I like her."

"Don't get too comfy," I warn.

"Antonio, my life is in Italy and not America. She and I would never work, but that doesn't mean we can't indulge a little while we're here. I promise I'm being a complete gentleman."

With Stefano, there's no such thing as being a gentleman, but I don't argue the point. I refuse to spend the weekend fighting or worrying about what two grown people are doing in private. I have enough on my hands with Lauren and making sure she's happy and relaxing as I'd hoped.

"You and Lauren seem to be doing well."

"We are."

We're better than well, but I don't get into details with Stefano. He's always been on a need-to-know basis, and right now, he doesn't need to know everything when it comes to my life with Lauren.

"Are you moving to America? Mamma says you're rarely home anymore."

"I don't know. The merger has kept me in the States longer than I had planned. And being with Lauren doesn't make it easy for me to get away, but once everything settles down..."

"She's okay with moving to Italy?" he asks before I can finish the sentence.

"I don't know. We haven't discussed it. The relationship is still new, Stefano. We're taking baby steps."

"You've been in American too long. You're starting to talk like one. What man says baby steps?"

"Shut up with your Italian macho bravado bullshit. Wait until you fall in love, and we'll see how long it is before you're on your knees, begging her for a taste."

"I never beg."

"Mm-hm," I mumble.

I hope I can live long enough to see the day that someone makes Stefano beg and puts him in his place.

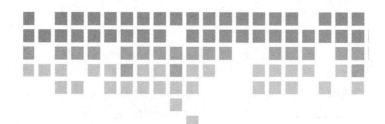

Chapter 19

Lauren

"Ouch." Tara turns and glares at Stefano as they sit on the edge of the deck. "Lighter."

Tara's skin color matches the lobster we just ate for dinner. I told her to wear sunscreen, but being the stubborn person she is, she didn't even bother. She gave me a line about her Italian ancestry and how the sun never caused her skin to burn. But this is the Caribbean, and even a pure-blooded Italian can burn.

"When I'm done, can you get my back?" Stefano asks her as he rubs the aloe on her shoulders, but this time much softer.

"Finish me, and I'll take care of you."

Stefano and Tara are a matching pair with their red skin and bullheaded attitudes. But they seem to work in the oddest way. Tara already told me that Stefano has tried to get the upper hand, trying to control every aspect of their time together. She quickly put him in his place and taught him how American women handle themselves. Surprisingly, she hasn't scared him away, and he's still panting after her like a little puppy dog.

He leans over her back but is careful not to touch her skin as he places his mouth next to her ear. "God, that sounds so sexy coming from your lips."

Antonio peeks over the counter and smiles at me from inside the house. "Who wants something to drink?"

"Vodka." I point at myself and decide I'm not going to spend our last night on the island stone-cold sober watching Stefano and Tara make goo-goo eyes at each other.

"Let's have lemon drops," Tara says over her shoulder, giving me a devilish smile.

Shit. I haven't done lemon drop shots since college, and the last time, I vowed never to do them again. I've spent so many years devoted to my work and not having fun with friends while they barhopped and slept around that I quickly make up my mind.

"I'm in."

"What is this lemon drop you speak of?" Stefano asks as he pours more aloe into his palm.

"It's sin in a glass, baby." Tara smiles at Stefano before shooting me a wink.

"Sounds perfect."

"Let's play a drinking game too."

I glance upward, already regretting my call for vodka. "What's that?"

The cultural differences between our Italian companions aren't really that noticeable until times like this. I'm sure Antonio was exposed to drinking games in college because frat boys are the same all over the world. But Stefano...he's an entirely different case. I can't imagine the Mafioso sit around coming up with childish reasons to down liquor in quantities that could be deadly.

"Well." Tara taps her chin and pauses. "It's where you play a game, and then you have to drink."

"Americans are so strange," Stefano says with a small laugh. "Why do you need a reason to drink?"

"Come on, No-No. Don't be a party pooper."

I almost fall off my chair when she calls him No-No. I cover my mouth and hide my laughter as she continues.

"It'll be fun. I promise. That is, unless you're scared you are going to lose."

She threw down the gauntlet. A man like Stefano doesn't like smack talk, especially when it comes from a woman. She knew exactly what she was doing when she spoke those words. They feed off each other, and for some odd reason, I find it amusing.

Antonio sits down next to me with a bottle of vodka in his hand as he stares at Stefano and Tara. "This is going to be trouble."

"You up for it, Forte?" I lift an eyebrow and take a page out of Tara's book with a little trash-talking.

Antonio smiles as he sets the bottle of vodka down on the table in front of him. "Mi amore, my baby bottle was filled with wine. I think I can handle anything you girls can throw at me."

I twist my lips and laugh.

"We're playing Never Have I Ever," Tara announces.

"Ugh," I groan. It's my least favorite drinking game.

"Don't pussy out, Lauren. It'll be fun. We may learn a thing or two about these guys."

She has a point. There's so much I still don't know about Antonio because they're not things you can come right out and ask. But maybe after a few rounds, I'll learn more than I ever cared to know.

"Bring it." I snap my fingers and pray I don't regret this in the morning

▪ ▪ ▪ ▪ ▪ ▪ ▪

We're six questions in, sitting around a table on the wraparound deck, and we've all had enough drinks to call it a night. That was if we were playing any normal game without the smack talk that got the ball rolling. I already know I'll be cursing Tara under my breath. We have a long trip home, and the last thing I want to do is spend it curled up on the couch, praying for death.

"Okay. So..." Tara straightens in her chair and glances around the table. "Never have I ever had a threesome."

I raise an eyebrow because I know Tara has had sex with more than one person. "Aren't you supposed to say something you haven't done?"

"It wasn't a threesome." She grins. "Technically, it was a foursome. You should know this."

The vivid descriptions she'd given me come flooding back. She's right; she was the fourth person in that group. I teased her for weeks afterward, but damn if I didn't fantasize about being there in her place.

Stefano has his glass halfway to his lips when he turns to her with the biggest eyes. "Three other women?" He sounds so hopeful and turned on.

"Sorry, buddy. Three men."

Stefano slams back his drink and sets the glass on the table before leaning over to whisper in Tara's ear. She laughs, turning to stare into his eyes after he speaks. I don't know what he said, but it made her face turn a whole new shade of red.

I peer over at Antonio and his empty glass. I'd been so wrapped up in Stefano and Tara that I hadn't seen him drink. But I'm not surprised the man has been in a threesome. I'm quite certain, based on his past, that he's had more than one.

"Drink the shot, Lauren." Tara turns her attention to me because the bitch knows too many of my secrets.

I can feel Antonio's eyes on me as I down my shot and slam the glass to the table. "What?" I say, feeling defensive. "It was college, and I experimented."

I shouldn't take offense at the stares. It's not like any of them didn't drink. They've all been in a group sexual situation, but I guess since it's me, somehow it seems outlandish.

"Man or woman?" Antonio asks as I turn to face him. "For the third?"

"It was me and another woman with a man."

Antonio rubs his chin as his eyes flicker down my body. "I figured."

"You?"

"Man," he says quickly.

I raise my eyebrows, wondering what that deliciousness would be like. Antonio with another man. Gah. It's more than my brain can process at once.

Stefano raises his hand. "He's sitting right here as proof."

My eyes drift between the two of them, and my mind spins out of control. Maybe it's the vodka or the fact that someone banged the brothers together, but my thoughts are everywhere.

"Whoa." Tara's eyes are almost bugged out of her sockets, matching my sentiments exactly. "That's kinda freaky even for me."

"Why?" Stefano asks.

I stare at Antonio, dumbfounded. He smiles with an easy shrug but says nothing more.

"'Cause he's your brother. I don't ever want to see my sister naked." Tara pretends to vomit under the table. "It's just...ew."

Stefano laughs as he covers her hand with his own. "It's not like I haven't seen his dick before. I have the same exact one, love."

"Was it just some random girl?"

I almost want to tell Tara to be quiet. I don't want to hear anything more because, well, we're talking about my boyfriend's sex life. But then, we're talking about his sex life, a sex life I didn't know about, and I'm more interested to hear the answer than I should be.

"No. We dated during our last year of high school. It was graduation night, and we drank a little too much. One thing led to another and, well..."

"What a lucky cunt," Tara says, looking down between Stefano's legs. "You two ruined her for life."

"My turn!" I yell, a little louder than I anticipated because all the threesome talk has made me uncomfortable and a little turned on.

"Fill your glasses, bitches." I push the bottle of vodka forward and wait for Stefano to pour the next round. I glance over at Antonio and rest my hand on his leg. "Having fun?" I ask him because I'm torn between this being the best night spent with friends in a long time or the most awkward experience with my best friend and boyfriend ever.

Antonio stares back at me with a look I can't quite place. Maybe he's embarrassed about his brother, but they were kids. I did some stupid shit at eighteen too. I wasn't too far into my freshman year when I agreed to have sex with my then-boyfriend and another woman. I never thought they'd end up falling for each other and I'd be left out in the cold. In all honesty, he and I weren't serious and had only gone on three official dates when he broached the topic. I should've run like the wind, but I thought, what the hell? Gotta try everything at least once.

"It's okay. I'm having fun," I tell him and squeeze his leg. "Be ready, Forte. I'm coming for you." I smile.

I lift my glass and peer around the table as they stare at me, waiting. There are so many possibilities. So many things I want to know, but I also don't want to willingly incriminate myself either. This is about finding out their secrets and not divulging my own. "Never have I ever been arrested." I smile because, hell, I've never been in any trouble with the law.

In unison, they lift their glasses to their lips and down the vodka before reaching for a lemon to wash it down. I add that to the growing list of things I didn't know about Antonio.

This night is turning out to be full of surprises.

Antonio

Lauren can barely stand up without my help. She's toppled over twice, and we're not even three feet away from the table.

Tara's no better as Stefano carries her toward the guesthouse, and she's singing a very off-key version of "Welcome to the Jungle" by Guns N' Roses.

"Is an animal dying?" Lauren asks as she stares up at me with glassy eyes.

"It's Tara, mi amore." I lift her into my arms because I don't want to spend an hour helping her make it to the bed. "She's singing."

She rests her head on my chest and sighs. "I wish you'd carry me like this always. It's so much easier than walking."

"Are you okay?"

She's a little more carefree than she usually is, but that's usually her way after so many drinks. Although Lauren's been drunk in front of me before, even the first night we met, she's way past her limit. Tomorrow, she's going to be miserable.

I place her on the bed, and she sprawls out with her arms and legs wide, looking almost angelic. "Leave me here to die," she whispers with her eyes closed.

"Are you relaxed?" I try not to laugh. The plan for this weekend was relaxation, and right now, she's nothing but a pool of jelly. No, that's not right. She probably has a higher vodka content in her body than water.

"I'm comatose."

She starts to giggle softly, and her eyes flutter open. She stares down the length of her body where I'm standing over her, watching in complete amusement. "Get undressed."

I raise an eyebrow and smirk. "I'm going to clean up outside. Why don't you get some rest, and I'll be to bed in a bit?"

With more deftness than I expect from a woman in her state, she climbs to her knees and places her hands on my chest. She bats her eyelashes as she uses her fingernails to trace my pec. "Take off your shorts. I don't want to ask twice."

"Love, I don't think you're in any condition to..."

She covers my mouth with her hand and leans forward. "You're not my daddy. Strip and present yourself."

I touch her shoulder, holding back my laughter at her stern sexy talk. "Where's your whip?"

"I gotta a hand to spank you," she slurs.

She sways, and I release her shoulders, letting her body fall backward onto the bed. Before she can say another word, I undo the button on my shorts and push them to the floor.

My cock is ready, standing at attention and pointing right at her. I like the frisky side of Lauren, where she takes charge. I don't know if it's the liquor talking tonight, but I'm not going to try to talk her out of it again.

"Come here." She motions with her hands, still lying flat on her back but staring down her body at me.

I climb onto the bed, inching my way up between her legs with the biggest smile because she can barely focus and will most likely pass out before we even start to fuck.

"Not like that. Climb up here. I want to suck that beautiful cock."

I straddle her waist, careful not to crush her with my knees as I move forward. "On your back?"

Her face grows serious. "Don't question me."

I hover over her chest with my cock just inches from her mouth. She licks her lips and places her warm hands on my ass, groping me roughly.

"You're always ready, Forte."

I place my hands on my hips, letting my cock bob in her face. When it comes to Lauren, I'm always ready for anything she has to offer, especially when she wants to suck my dick.

I can tell the angle is all wrong. The only thing I'll be doing is smacking the roof of her mouth. I grab a pillow and lift her head, all while my cock is doing a mad dash for her lips like it has a mind of its own.

She wraps her tiny hands around my shaft and yanks me forward. "Closer," she says in a deep, sultry tone.

I'd laugh at her behavior if my cock weren't so close to her teeth and she weren't drunk. I inch forward, careful not to suffocate her, but I don't see how this is going to work with her hand-to-eye coordination at record lows.

"Lauren, I..."

Her snore echoes through the room as her hand falls away from my ass and plops on the bed to her side. The ride was good while it lasted. It could've been sexy if she were sober, but I know that tomorrow she's going to be in more pain than I am now.

I climb off the bed and adjust her so she's lying down the length of the bed instead of having her feet dangle off the edge.

The weekend hasn't been a total bust. Lauren and Tara had fun, even though a majority of it was alcohol-induced. If nothing else, we learned more about each other, and I felt like my brother was finally turning a corner in his life.

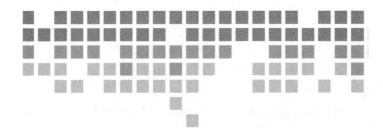

Chapter 20

Lauren

I've decided that the sun in the Caribbean is far too bright. Even with my darkest pair of sunglasses, I can't open my eyes fully because the glare is more than I can bear. The tiny jackhammer inside my head is a constant reminder of the amount of vodka I drank last night. I barely remember getting to bed, but I have a vivid image of Antonio's cock in my face before I fell asleep.

"Thank you for a wonderful time," Stefano says as he wraps his arms around his brother while we stand outside the airport in Nassau.

I pull the brim of my beach hat down a little farther, trying to shade my eyes more, but it's no use. Any amount of light is too much at this point.

Tara isn't faring any better than me. If she weren't so sunburnt, I'd swear her new shade was green. We smack-talked our way into the world's worst hangover, and this is God's way of paying us back.

"I'm happy you joined us. Maybe we can do this again sometime."

"No vodka though, 'kay?" Tara grabs her head and sways.

Stefano reaches out and steadies her. "This is all my fault."

She grips his arms and stares at him under the brim of her hat. "It's not my first hangover, Stefano. I'm a big girl."

"Maybe we can do this again sometime." The poor guy looks so hopeful when he makes the statement, but I know my girl, and she probably won't dip her foot in that well again.

"We'll see. I have a pretty busy schedule."

"I like a woman who plays hard to get."

Tara laughs briefly. "Damn, this is horrible." She grabs her head again and lets out a little whimper. "I may never drink again."

I feel the same way, but we both know it would be a lie.

Stefano pulls her hand away from her head and kisses her fingers first before making his way to her wrist. "Until next time, Tara. It was a pleasure."

A hint of a smile crosses her face, but too much is hidden by her sunglasses and hat. We'll be having a conversation once we've both recovered so I can find out exactly what happened this weekend.

Before Stefano walks away, he gives me a kiss on each cheek and says, "I enjoyed the weekend with you, Lauren. I'm excited you'll be part of the family."

I freeze, and my sunglasses-covered gaze finds Antonio. He looks as shocked as I am by Stefano's words, so I ignore the comment and give him a light pat on the back. "The weekend turned out better than I expected."

Minus the hangover. The first night I was wound a little too tight, worried for my friend because I had forgotten she could handle her own. The Stefano who came to the island is one I could love. Not the same way I do Antonio, but someone I could respect as family.

Stefano walks away and reaches for his phone. Before he disappears into the building, Tara's phone chimes, and Stefano flashes her a smile.

"You gave him your number?" I ask.

"Maybe." She smirks.

Her big talk of not seeing him again and playing hard to get was all an act. The little minx couldn't resist the charms of Stefano Forte even if he behaved like an asshole.

"We're not dating, but I'd fuck him again for sure," she says as she types him a reply.

I shrug, too exhausted for anything else and feeling a bit like roadkill. "I'm ready to go home."

"Your chariot awaits," Antonio says and motions toward the private runway to the right of the main terminal.

There's definitely an upside to flying in a private jet. I couldn't handle a crowd right now. Especially with the evil little person that's chipping away pieces of my skull as a constant reminder of last night's stupidity.

Tara hooks her arm with mine as we walk toward the tarmac. "These Forte men are something else, huh?"

"Just watch yourself. I hated Antonio when I met him, and look where I am now."

"Jet-setting all over the world and in love with a guy packing a ten-inch pecker?"

I can't help it. I crack up and hold my head, wincing through the pain until it turns into tears. "I hate you sometimes," I tell her as we climb the stairs to the jet with Antonio behind us.

"But you're stuck with me forever."

"I wouldn't have it any other way."

Antonio

Lauren's lying in the bed and checking her emails, almost recovered from the vodka and airplane ride. She glances up from her screen and smiles softly.

"I was thinking about this weekend," I say as I settle in next to her.

She sets her phone down and gives me her full attention. "Which part?"

"It was right before you passed out."

Her eyes widen.

"My cock was..."

She buries her face in her hands and groans. "I'm so embarrassed."

I pull her hands away from her face. "I'm kidding. I never expected anything to happen. You were so drunk, but you were superbossy. Kind of how I'd think you'd be as a boss."

"Bossy? In the bedroom?"

"You threatened to spank me." I smirk as her face turns a lovely shade of red.

She sinks down into the pillow and hides her face. "This is mortifying."

"If that's your thing, I'm game."

"Right now?"

I shake my head. "Whenever you want."

"Oh God, don't ever let me drink that much again."

I laugh and pull her into my arms as I lie down. "I wasn't really thinking about that. We'll forget it ever happened."

I won't forget. It's a memory I'll keep forever. Even when we're old and gray, I'll remember it.

"And the spanking?"

"That we'll talk about another day."

"Are you into that?" she asks, stroking her favorite spot on my chest.

"I'm into anything you are."

She peers up at me with questioning eyes. "Change the subject, please."

"I wanted to talk about what Stefano said."

I'd been dancing around the topic for hours. I knew the words struck her as odd when Stefano said them at the airport before he walked inside the terminal. He had asked me if I intended to ask Lauren for her hand in marriage, and I'd told him she was the first woman I had even considered doing so.

"Stefano broached a subject I've thought about in the last week."

Her hand stills. "Okay."

I cover her hand with mine and glance down. "Let's say someday we get married. Where will we live?"

It's a fair question. I remember Lauren telling me she'd live nowhere else besides Chicago. She said she needed the grit of the city like she needed air. Although I like the city, I could never live here full time.

"I don't know," she mumbles, snuggling her cheek against my chest. "I haven't thought about it."

"I own a home in Italy, and you have this penthouse in Chicago."

"Would we have to pick one or the other?"

I've never stayed in one place too long. Work has kept me on the move for over a decade, but the travel is starting to wear on me.

"Not at first," I concede. "But someday, if we have children, we couldn't travel as easily. They need stability."

She pushes herself up and stares at me with a look I haven't seen before. "Whoa. Whoa. Whoa. You're talking about babies I give birth to?"

"Yeah." I touch her nose and smile. God, our children would be the most beautiful little things in the world. I could almost picture them laughing and running around our...yard? Kids can't grow up in a penthouse surrounded by cement and metal. They need room to play, to grow, to explore.

"When should I fit that in? In between billion-dollar business deals? Just say, hey, can we put this on hold while I squeeze out a mini Forte?"

"You can take time off. You're not the first female CEO on the planet."

Her eyes narrow. "I don't think I'm quite ready to have kids."

"I'm not saying we're having them tomorrow, but we have to think ahead."

"Maybe that's better left to chance." She falls back down in my arms with a loud huff.

"I want children someday, Lauren. I want an entire army of little people with our eyes and noses. I want that with you."

Never have I wanted anything more. Six months ago, children and marriage weren't even on my radar. But being with Lauren and falling in love has changed everything.

"I'll stay home and take care of them," I say because I'm a fucking idiot. I can't take care of kids by myself, but I'd say anything to make my dream a reality.

"Can we talk about this tomorrow?"

I settle into the bed and pull her closer. "Yes, but we're going to have to face our future sooner or later."

"I'm still hungover and exhausted. I need to sleep, or I'll be useless at the office. While it's nice to talk about the relationship future, if this merger falls apart, there won't be much of anything happening for a long time."

I kiss her forehead and close my eyes. "Everything will turn out fine. Sleep, and we'll talk about it another time."

She slings her leg over mine and cozies up in her favorite position. My hand sweeps up and down her back as I stare at the ceiling and think about our future. Two workaholics, living on different continents.

What could possibly go wrong?

Chapter 21

Two Months Later

Lauren

"Congratulations." Mr. Grayson smiles as he shakes my hand. "I now have more money than I know what to do with."

"Sir, you had that before the merger was finalized," I remind him.

"Maybe I'll finally retire and learn to play golf." He laughs, the apples of his cheeks almost kissing his eyes.

Mr. Grayson is well into his seventies, but he has never been one to sit around. He's never missed a board meeting and has always had my back. If he retired, I'd miss his presence in the boardroom, and no one would ever be able to take his place.

"By the way, did you ever figure out who sold us out to Cozza?"

I give him a pained smile. "I did, sir, and they're being dealt with before the end of business today."

"Good. I have full faith that you'll do the right thing, my dear," he says before he walks out of the boardroom with Tad Connors at his side.

For the first time since I met him, Tad didn't ask a single question before the paperwork was finalized with Cozza. I think all the zeros that were added to his bank account left him speechless.

"Wonderful job, Ms. Bradley." Ms. Edwards tries to smile, but her face is so tight from a new surgery that she looks like she's eaten something sour. "I'm sure Stanton is weeping himself to sleep tonight. Poor thing."

I snicker because her husband, Stanton, was truly an asshole. He was a member of the good ol' boys club that treated women like shit. I had the pleasure of working with him for a few years, and I celebrated the day he stepped down as CEO after practically being forced out by the board.

"I wouldn't be here without him."

She laughs exuberantly with an arm raised as she dips backward on one leg. "Thank you for doing something my husband never could."

"What's that, Ms. Edwards?"

"Make me happy." She smirks that painful, face-pulling smirk before she saunters out the door of the conference room in the most beautiful pair of Louboutins.

Antonio is standing across the room, shaking hands with members of his board just as I have been doing with mine. There's still allegiances that need to be broken and rebuilt because we started out as enemies, but we need to find a way to become a single entity that goes deeper than the company name.

I dip my head to him with a small smile as he shakes the hand of Mr. Alesci, a member of Cozza's legal team. Antonio returns the gesture with a small wink, and it suddenly becomes as hot as a summer day in the air-conditioned boardroom, which usually feels more like a meat locker down at the stockyards.

I watch him stalk my way once the room empties, and my heart does a flip-flop. The man still steals my breath somehow, at least once a day. Even though I've avoided the subject of marriage and kids, I can't imagine being with anyone else.

"Are you ready for this?"

I nod, but I'm not sure I am.

After the deal was set in stone and the merger was happening no matter what, Antonio finally revealed the identity of the mole. It wasn't easy to get the name out of him either. He wanted to wait, but I reminded him about the sheet of paper he'd signed in my office when he waved the proposition in my face that started us down the path to merging our corporations in the first place.

I was beyond shocked to find out who had ratted us out to the executives at Cozza, but they say anyone is willing to stab you in the back if the price is high enough.

"Let's get it over with. Rip the Band-Aid off."

Antonio had become better with his English, picking up funny phrases and using them way too much, but I never minded because they typically made me smile.

We walk together toward my office with our hands almost touching. We haven't been able to hide our relationship. Word spread quickly when we started to take too many trips together. The backlash was almost nonexistent after we reassured all parties that it would in no way affect the merger or how the company was run in the future.

I earned my place as CEO. I worked my ass off and brought a new engine to market that will revolutionize the entire industry. No one could deny it. I didn't sleep my way to the top or buy my way on to the board. I earned my position through blood, sweat, and tears, and nothing could ever change that.

Cassie looks up from her desk as we approach, with the biggest smile on her face. "Is it done?"

"It is. We're officially Cozza Interstellar Corp, CIC for short."

She leans back and spins around in her chair, filled with excitement. "I'm buying myself a Lexus."

Antonio and I glance at each other and laugh.

"Bought some shares, did you?"

"I've been socking away shares since the day Ms. Bradley became CEO. I knew this woman was going to make me rich."

Suddenly, I feel panicked. "You aren't quitting, are you?"

"Not yet. We have work to do, Ms. Bradley."

Antonio pulls a yellow envelope from inside his suit jacket and hands it to Cassie after I give him the signal that it's time to finally drop some dead weight.

She glances at the front, and her eyes widen. "You want me to..."

"File the papers, and then tell him to come to my office at once," I say and take a deep breath because this is going to be one of the hardest things I've ever done.

"Yes, ma'am." She picks up the phone and taps a few buttons as Antonio leads me into my office.

When I found out there was a mole inside my company, everyone was a suspect, even Cassie. As she worked the closest with me, she knew more than most people in the company. It would've made sense for her to sell secrets to the competitor because she could make a lifetime's worth of money in a single shot. But Cassie didn't sell me out. No. She's always had my back, and her loyalty will be rewarded.

But the one person who did stab me in the back is about to have his tenure with Cozza Interstellar severed forever.

■ ■ ■ ■ ■ ■ ■ ■

Antonio stands beside my chair with his arms folded in front of his chest, looking rather imposing. "Have a seat," he says.

"What's this about?" He looks to Antonio and then back to me. "I was in the middle of something important."

"Josh." I clear my throat and lean forward with my hands clasped in front of me on the desk. "It has come to my attention that you were behind the leak to Cozza."

Josh. The weasel. Not only did he give away top secret information, but more than once during the merger, he tried to take my future position within the new company.

He snarls, and his eyes flash with anger. "I did no such thing," he snaps at me.

Antonio places his hand on my chair and takes a step forward, but I hold my hand up and stop his advance. "I have a signed affidavit from Chloe Cantrell, a past employee at Cozza, which says you gave her the intel that started the entire takeover to begin with."

"Who?" He scoots forward in his chair and plays coy. "Why would I do such a stupid thing?"

"Ms. Cantrell had quite the story to tell about you, Mr. Goldman," Antonio adds, and I can almost hear the smirk in his voice.

"It's all lies!"

I pull out the piece of paper and push it toward Josh so that he can read the words for himself. He snatches it off the desk before I have a chance to remove my hand and starts to scan the words.

I lean back, watching him carefully as his eyes grow wider with each sentence. The tale she had to tell was damning both professionally and personally. Josh's wife had just had their third child, and for something like this to come out would be devastating.

Antonio told me the entire gory story in very vivid detail, and when I didn't believe it, he gave me the affidavit so I could read it with my own eyes. Carlino, the VP at Cozza, put the entire thing into motion, and Josh stepped right into the trap he'd set. They'd watched numerous people within my company, looking for someone who had a weak spot they could exploit in order to gain insider information.

Josh was the victim of their scheme, but he could have come to me, and we would've found a way to fix it. Instead, he sold out Interstellar and gave an Oscar-worthy performance when they started their dawn takeover raid.

I, Chloe Cantrell, willingly took part in a scheme to extract information from Mr. Josh Goldman of Interstellar Corp. Upon gaining part-time employment at the Pleasure Den, I was to take Mr. Goldman on as a new client inside. In my position as a dominatrix and in the process of serving his needs, I was to take incriminating photos to be used later against Mr. Goldman to facilitate the extraction of information.

I had five sessions with Mr. Goldman in the month that he became my slave. While he was my submissive who was turned on by humiliation, I used the opportunity to photograph and film our sessions as proof, at the request of Carlino Sosa. After the five sessions and gathering more than enough information, I terminated my sexual relationship with Mr. Goldman along with my employment at the Pleasure Den.

After waiting three months, I called Mr. Goldman and set up a meeting. He was more than eager to see me again, but he wasn't aware of the reason for the meeting. Instead of going myself, Mr. Sosa met with Mr. Goldman and showed him the photos and video. Mr. Goldman was told that if he didn't provide information on what Interstellar was working on, a photograph a day would be mailed to his wife, along with clips from the lengthy video session.

Fearing that his secret would be exposed, not only for the sake of his family but also because of the sensitive nature of his sexual proclivities, Mr. Goldman cooperated without hesitation and furnished Mr. Sosa with the information, thus ending my communication with Mr. Goldman.

"Mr. Sosa and Ms. Cantrell have both been let go," Antonio says as he moves to the front of my desk. "Your office is being packed right now, and you'll be escorted off the premises as soon as you leave this office."

"Lauren." Josh leans forward, gripping the paper so tightly it crumples in his fingers. "Let me explain, please," he begs.

If he would've come to me, I would've helped him. I could have given him something to hand over to Cozza that would've satisfied them and taken the heat off him long enough for us to find a way to salvage his reputation and career.

"There's nothing to explain. The damage is done. You should've come to me, and I would've helped you."

I'd do anything to shield my employees and stop any catastrophe from coming down on the shoulders of my company. Whether they're willing to ask for the assistance because they need to save their own asses is their choice.

He's pale and hunched over, almost hyperventilating.

"The photos have been destroyed and will never see the light of day. Mr. Sosa and Ms. Cantrell have both signed nondisclosure agreements, and if they break the NDA, they will lose more money than they're willing to part with. So your secret sexual escapades are safe and shall never be revealed by any of the parties involved."

Antonio sits at the edge of my desk and stares down at Josh. He's kept himself composed and let me run the meeting for the most part. I expected him to take control, but once again, Mr. Forte surprised me.

"You will be given a small severance package and must cash out your stock immediately. Based on the number of shares you own, you'll never need to work again."

"But..."

I hold up my hand, stopping him from saying another word. "There's nothing more to say. You are a traitor to the company and will be blackballed in the industry. If you apply for a job, I will tell your potential new employer why you were let go. Be wise and retire young. I should have your ass thrown in jail."

"No, don't." He stands quickly and glances at Antonio. "I'll go." He walks toward the door and stares down at the floor. Before he leaves, he turns to me and says, "I'm sorry, Lauren. I really am."

"Me too, Josh. Me too."

He leaves without another word. Security is outside my office waiting for him. They escort him to the elevator without any problem. The entire office has stopped, and everyone's watching him as he waits for a car to arrive.

"I almost feel bad for the guy," I whisper as Antonio stands just inside the doorway, and I watch as Josh waits.

"We make our own choices, and now he has to deal with the consequences. It's not like he's walking out of here empty-handed. He's a millionaire many times over."

"You're right, but that doesn't help ease my nerves over the entire situation."

The fact that Josh profited from his deception is sickening. He would've been this wealthy if our new invention had come to market without any hiccups, and he'd still be employed at Interstellar.

But I don't let myself go there. Looking back and wanting a do-over would mean that I wouldn't have Antonio by my side. That thought is unbearable because he's become just as much a part of my life as my work had been.

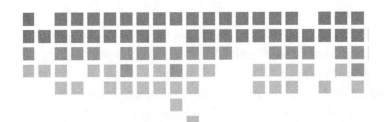

Chapter 22

Antonio

The first full day as Cozza Interstellar has started better than I expected. Morale seems to be up across the board, and not one person has uttered a snide remark in my presence. The company is still being housed on two separate campuses while a new world headquarters is being built only a few miles away on the outskirts of Chicago.

Lauren's fitting in with the people at Cozza and has easily filled my shoes. She came in with guns blazing, and I think she frightened more than a few people with her don't-give-a-shit attitude. I couldn't be prouder of her and everything she's accomplished with so many cards stacked against her.

Last night after we left the office, she didn't want to go out to celebrate. Instead, we visited her parents' graves so she could tell them the news. I stayed by the car, watching her as she wept over their grassy plots in order to give her the space she requested.

Before we left, I took a moment and went to pay my respects alone. But I wasn't there to say something random. I wanted to tell Lauren's parents that I would be looking out for her. I went as far as to ask her father if I could have her hand in marriage even though I knew he couldn't reply. If he were here, I would've done the same thing. In some ways, I'm old-fashioned, and I know that her parents' opinion would mean a lot.

After I said my piece, I joined her in the car and took her back to her penthouse for a quiet evening by the fireplace. There was no major celebration or fanfare. The day which was both filled with joy and excitement was dampened by having to fire her previous second-in-command.

I knew how she felt. Having to let go of anyone was awful, but doing it to someone you're close with is beyond compare. I felt nothing the day I fired Carlino. No. That's a lie. I felt a sense of relief that I no longer had to look over my shoulder, waiting to see the light glimmer off the shiny blade he was about to stick in my back.

Standing outside Lauren's office now, I take a moment to glance around the floor and watch our new employees at work. They're buzzing with excitement as they place calls and say the words Cozza Interstellar Corp. No other company can match our power and wealth, especially now that the Mercury engine is in full production and every airline company in the world has ordered enough planes to replace their entire fleet within the next ten years.

On top of that, NASA has contracted CIC to fit their newest rockets with the Mercury so that they can begin testing its power and endurance for a possible trip to Mars within the decade. Although I want to take credit, the entire thing is because of Lauren. Her drive to succeed and make her father proud has brought us to this very moment and place.

Loud voices coming from inside her office draw my attention away from the employee chatter. I don't knock. I press my ear against the door, eavesdropping. I know Lauren would have my balls if she caught me.

"Be reasonable," a man says. "Do what's right for the company and step down."

I lean closer and grab the handle, ready to storm inside and save the day, but something makes me stop and wait.

"Get the fuck out of my office!" Lauren yells.

"You don't deserve to be the head of this company. Forte only stepped down because you're fucking him. Under any other circumstances, do you really think he'd do that?"

I storm through the door and lunge at Jim Alesci, the head legal counsel for Cozza. He jumps back, but he trips over a chair, making it easy for me to wrap my fingers around his neck. "You fucking piece of shit." Spit flies out of my mouth, landing on his face below me. "I will fucking end you."

Jim struggles under my fingers, but I'm not trying to kill him. I've already done enough physical damage to easily be removed as COO of the company, but I take stock in knowing he won't be around either.

"Do you suck her dick, Antonio?" he bites out as I resist the urge to kill him.

Lauren pulls at my jacket, trying to get me off of him, but he knocks her out of the way with his leg while he's trying to get free. She loses her balance and topples to the floor near Jim's feet.

I stand and lift him off the floor with me. I pull my fist back, ready to strike when Lauren grabs my arm. "Don't," she says, pleading with me for this asshole.

I turn to her, tightening my grip on Jim's shirt. "Why? The bastard deserves at least a black eye."

"He's not worth it," she says, calm and very matter-of-fact. "Please."

Slowly, I release my tight grip and push him backward. "Get your shit and get out of here. You're no longer an employee of CIC."

His eyes narrow, and his nostrils flare. "You can't do this. I'll make you pay for this."

"Sue me, Jim. I'm sure the courts would love to hear the sexual harassment suit we'll bring against you."

He straightens his arms at his sides and glares at both of us. "I will make you pay."

I wave him off because Jim talks the talk, but the man most certainly does not walk the walk. Never have I seen him lay into even a low-level employee before, let alone a member of the board. I wonder how many other employees he's accosted without my knowledge for fear they'd be fired if they reported it.

Lauren

I expected some backlash after I officially took the helm at Cozza Interstellar, but I never expected it to be from someone on the legal team and a valued friend of Antonio's.

Jim had never shown one ounce of animosity toward me over the last few months. He didn't even look at me sideways or make any remarks that could be construed as derogatory.

I don't know what changed that made him march into my office and demand my resignation. He didn't have the authority to do it, and I wasn't going to back down for some asshole who thought he could hustle me right out of a job.

"I'm sorry," I say as soon as Jim walks out and slams my door behind him.

Antonio turns toward me and wraps his arms around my waist, pulling me close. "For what?"

I close my eyes and press my face into his suit jacket. "Everything is a mess right now."

"No, it's not. Don't listen to that prick. You're exactly where you should be."

"I'm sure other people are saying the same thing behind my back."

Maybe not the women within the company, but ninety percent of males are probably at least thinking the same thing as Jim, but they have enough sense not to utter the words to my face.

No matter how many glass ceilings are shattered, there will always be one misogynistic asshole to throw some bullshit in a woman's face.

Antonio grabs my shoulders and holds me at a distance, gazing into my eyes. "No matter what they think, I never brought an invention to market that will revolutionize the entire aerospace industry the way you did. Don't let one asshole destroy everything you've worked so hard to achieve."

"I know," I mumble before exhaling because I'm still filled with doubt. "But I don't know if I can do this."

I doubt myself like I never have before. Running Interstellar was one thing. I came up through the ranks and learned the ropes, especially which men to steer clear of over the years, but adding Cozza's people to the mix puts me in virgin territory.

"You can do this."

If Antonio and I weren't in a relationship, I probably wouldn't feel the same way. With him at my back, I believe everything will eventually work out and we'll be able to bring the company together to work as one. But doing that rests on my shoulders, and the burden is heavy.

"What if I don't want to?"

Antonio's eyebrows turn downward as his eyes search mine. "You don't mean that. You need to get away from the office for a little while."

"I do mean it." I step out of his arms and pace the length of my office. "I've been locked away in this office for years, toiling away around the clock to make Interstellar number one and invent something so grandiose that I'd leave my mark on history."

"And you've achieved that."

"But at what cost? If I hadn't met you in that bar months ago, I'd be alone, with a bottle of vodka and Tara as my closest confidants."

Antonio's shocked by my words, but they're sobering and true. Over the years, I've thought about my stamp on history and achieving my father's dream. And now that I've done everything I set out to do, what's the point?

"Let's go away for a few days and relax. Maybe after a weekend away from the city, you'll feel differently."

"I want to spend time with your family."

"You do?" He raises his eyebrows toward his hairline before his lips turn up in a smile.

"Yes. Your mother called this morning to congratulate me, and I'd like to spend time with her."

Over the last few months, Mrs. Forte has opened her arms as well as her house to me. Feeling lost like I do right now calls for a trip for a little perspective only a mother can give. Even if she didn't give birth to me, she has enough experience and kindness to help guide me on the right path.

"I'll get the jet prepped. We'll leave when you're ready."

I almost knock him over as I wrap my arms around his back. Although the ocean calls my name, my heart wants nothing more than to be surrounded by Antonio's loving yet loud family, where I don't have to worry about their opinions or judgment.

He presses his hands to my face, forcing me to look in his eyes. "I love you, Lauren." He smiles softly.

My heart flutters because even though he's said those same words a hundred times, it never gets old.

"I love you too, Antonio."

The words come easily to me now. I never thought I'd find someone who would take my breath away and challenge me at every turn, but somehow, I have him.

Antonio Forte makes me think all things are possible.

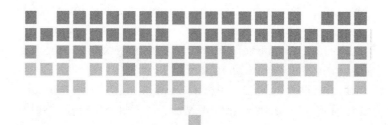

Chapter 23

Lauren

I gaze out the window, staring at the snow-covered tops of the Alps as we wind around the seemingly endless curves at their base. I felt reinvigorated as soon as we stepped off the plane into the warm, fragrant morning air, like I was where I was meant to be.

I never thought I could live anywhere else besides Chicago. I was born there, raised there, and it's the only place on earth that holds so many memories of my parents. But Italy has sucked me in, making me want the slower way of life where every moment is savored and nothing is wasted.

"My mother cooked all night," Antonio says as if I didn't already know that.

CHELLE BLISS

Mrs. Forte hasn't stopped her mission of trying to put some meat on my bones. She mutters the same words in Italian every time we're there about how frail I am and that she needs to take care of me.

To be honest, I love Antonio's family just as much as I love him. They've opened their arms to me and embraced me as one of their own without any reservations or hidden agendas. Even Stefano has grown on me, which I never thought would happen.

I glance toward Antonio and smile. My stomach rumbles at the thought of Mrs. Forte's cooking. "Will everyone be there?"

"No. Violetta is on tour in Germany with her band, and Flavia is somewhere in Norway in search of a Viking."

I chuckle as I imagine Flavia stalking through villages, trying to find the stereotypical Viking with facial hair and bulging muscles. "She knows they don't really exist anymore, right?"

He sighs. "She's been stalking some guy on Instagram for months. She claims he's the real thing and that she's just a fan, but I worry it's becoming an unhealthy obsession."

"We all love our fantasies. Let her live hers a little. She'll find out soon enough that the image we portray isn't always who we are."

"I suppose, mi amore."

As we pull into the familiar driveway, a sense of calm washes over me. Every bit of stress I have melts away every time we're here. That only happens in two places, and they're both near and dear to Antonio.

Mrs. Forte steps out the front door before the car comes to a complete stop and comes barreling down the stone stairway with the biggest smile on her face.

"I told you she was excited." He laughs as he places the car in park and turns off the engine.

Just like she does every time, she plucks me out of my seat and wraps me in a hug so tight, I almost lose my breath. "Ah, my dear. You are looking well." She pulls away and places her hands on my cheeks, giving them a hard pinch.

I wince and put my hands over hers, still not used to her pinching areas of my body to test my fragility. "It's so good to see you, Mamma." The name slides off my tongue like I was always meant to say the word to her.

"It's so good to have you home," she says as she pulls Antonio into our hug. "I know the girls are excited too."

"Where are they?" Antonio asks as his mother finally releases us.

"Sleeping. We didn't tell them you were coming so they wouldn't be awake at an ungodly hour. Come, let's have coffee on the veranda."

Antonio throws his arm around my shoulders as we follow his mother into the house. Catarina is outside, waiting for us with four mugs and a freshly brewed pot of coffee. The sun dances off the tiny ruffles on the water and twinkles as the breeze blows gently across the top. The view of the lake is more beautiful every time I see it.

Catarina rises from her chair with the biggest smile. "I'm so happy you're here this weekend. I needed someone to go shopping with. It's meant to be."

"It's a good thing I brought my credit cards," I laugh because Catarina makes shopping an Olympic sport.

"Sit. Sit," she says, opening her arms and motioning toward the chairs. "I want to hear about work."

I scrub my hand down my face, wanting to talk about anything but that. I'd rather stick hot pokers underneath my fingernails, but I decide to placate her with an easy answer. "The merger is done, and it's business as usual."

"That's it?" She glances toward Antonio with a perplexed look.

He shrugs and reaches for the coffeepot. "Everything's in place, but we've hit a few snags." He fills my cup and peers over at me before pouring his own. "But nothing we can't handle."

"Mamma," a tiny voice says behind me, and we all turn.

It's Amalia, standing just inside the house with her little bare feet inching toward the stone veranda as she rubs her eyes. She's wearing the cutest pink nightgown, with ruffles and lace lining the edges and skating across the floor.

"Mali," Antonio says and holds out his arms.

Her hand falls to her side, and her eyes grow wide. "Zio!" she squeals and runs across the patio in a mad dash before jumping into his arms.

"Ah, my girl. I've missed you," he whispers in her ear as she wraps her arms around his neck like a little monkey.

She pulls away and places her palms flat against his cheeks, squeezing until his lips pucker. "Zio Ant, I have so much to tell you." Her face is so serious as she speaks, and my heart flutters at the sight as Antonio smiles at her.

"Tell Zio Ant what's wrong, piccolo. I'll fix it."

The man would move mountains for those he loves, especially his nieces who have him wrapped around their little fingers. But in all reality, they have me too. All the hours spent playing and watching Toy Story on repeat haven't been for nothing. They lured me in, and there's no escaping their magical spell now.

"There's this boy," she whispers.

Antonio's eyes narrow, and he peers over at his sister. She lifts her hands and looks away. "I know. I know."

"She's seven for shit's sake."

Amalia gasps. "Zio, you can't say that word."

Antonio's face softens as he glances down at the little angel in his lap. "I'm sorry. What did this boy do?" He raises an eyebrow, and I'm wondering if he's already plotting against the boy.

"Well." She grabs ahold of his cheeks again and tilts her head, still with the most serious face I've ever seen on her. "We were on the swings, and he was pushing me."

"Did he knock you off?" Antonio jumps right to the worst-case scenario.

"No, Zio. Let me finish." Amalia takes control of the situation and puts her uncle in his place like she always does. "When the teacher called us back into the building, he helped me off the swing and then he kissed me."

Well, knocking Amalia off the swing would've been preferable to what she just told Antonio. His face turns a shade of red I haven't seen before, not even when Jim said the vilest things.

Antonio turns his gaze on his sister, who's smiling. "I will end him."

She laughs and rolls her eyes. "He's seven, brother. There's not much you can do about it."

"Zio. Listen. To. Me." Amalia's voice is so deep and husky that she immediately gets Antonio's attention.

"The teacher saw it and gave him a detention. But I don't understand."

"What don't you understand?" he bites out while his face is still smashed in her little hands.

"Why did he get in trouble? He didn't do anything wrong. I mean, you kiss Zia Lauren, and Pappa kisses Mamma, and no one puts you in detention."

"Mali, you're just a baby."

"I am not a baby. I'm seven."

I cover my mouth and chuckle quietly in my palm. Girls. We always want to grow up earlier than we should. I remember my first kiss and how in love I was with the boy who forever will be etched in my memory. It faded fast, especially when I caught him kissing my best friend by the monkey bars the very next day. It was my first failed relationship, but certainly not my last.

"I know. I know. But you're too young to kiss."

Her hands finally fall away from his face, and she crosses her arms in front of her chest, putting distance between them. "I am not too young. I liked it too," she says with so much sass.

Antonio's shell-shocked. His mouth opens like he's going to say something, but he can't decide what to say, so he snaps his lips shut. Amalia makes a face at him and hops off his lap before storming into the house.

"Well, I..." Antonio says, completely dumbfounded.

Mamma and Catarina are laughing almost to the point of crying because it's not very often that Antonio doesn't know how to handle a situation.

"We know," Catarina says. "I had the same talk with her yesterday. It's futile."

"I'm not ready for them to grow up."

"It's inevitable. I remember the first time you got in trouble for kissing a girl," Mamma says with a small laugh. "Her parents were so furious that her father pounded on our front door and demanded an apology."

"And so it begins," Antonio mutters.

"Wait until you have your own. It's so much worse," Catarina replies.

Antonio grimaces and glances in my direction. "We don't have to worry about that for some time. Lauren and I are taking it slow."

Mamma clears her throat and purses her lips. Her displeasure in the statement is evident. "Well, don't wait too long. Time isn't a luxury that comes with an infinite supply."

I learned that lesson with my parents. As a little girl, I thought I'd have them around forever. Death isn't something a child can comprehend, but I learned fast when my mother didn't come back. I cried at the front window in the living room for months, staring out the glass as I waited for her to return. In time, the cold, hard truth became my reality, but it wasn't until I was an adult that I finally understood the only thing that's infinite is death.

Antonio

Guila, Amalia, Catarina, and Lauren left two hours ago with fistfuls of cash and dozens of credit cards in their purses. They would most likely spend an amount equal to the GDP of some small nation and help boost the economy of Como in a single day.

"When are you going to ask her to marry you?" Mamma asks as I sit with her in the kitchen as she preps tonight's dinner.

"I've brought up the future, but Lauren wasn't ready to talk about it yet."

"Naturally, she wasn't. There was a lot going on between business and that mess with her ex-boyfriend. Everything is settled now, yes?"

"Yes, Mamma."

"Did you ask her to marry you?" She stares at me over the pot with her head tilted.

I shake my head and avert my eyes.

She places the spoon on the counter next to the pot of sauce that's already been cooking for hours, but that doesn't stop her from babying it until the taste is perfect. "No woman wants to talk about a hypothetical future. Ask her the question. If she loves you, she'll say yes. If she doesn't…"

"If she doesn't, what? Do I end the best and really only relationship I've ever had?"

"No." My mother covers my hand with hers. "If she says no, you ask again and again until she says yes."

"So, I pester her into marrying me?"

"I've spent enough time with Lauren to know she'll say yes. She's madly in love with you, but she is scared to take the next step. Remember, she's lost everyone she's ever loved. There's no greater heartache in the world than losing your parents. You should know this."

"I do."

"But you still have me and your brothers and sisters. Lauren has no one. She's been independent for so long that taking the next step has to be frightening."

"I suppose you're right, Mamma."

"I'm always right, Antonio." She smiles and pats my hand, going back to the pot of sauce and picking up her spoon. "Ask her. It's the only way you can move forward with certainty."

"I will."

"Now run to town and buy the biggest diamond you can find. Don't cut any corners, and make sure it's flawless."

I'm appalled that she thinks I'd get Lauren anything less, but it's my mother, and she always feels the need to "guide" her children.

I round the island and kiss her cheeks, thinking of everything I need to pull off a proposal that will make Lauren say yes without any hesitation. "I'll be back in a few hours."

"Big, Antonio," she says as I'm halfway to the door.

"Got it, Mamma!" I yell back and head into town, ready to spend a small fortune on a ring.

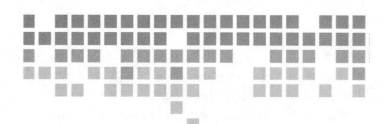

Chapter 24

Lauren

"Why didn't we eat with the rest of the family?" I ask as I set my fork down on my empty plate.

There's nothing better than Mrs. Forte's sauce. Not even the best restaurants in Chicago's Little Italy can come close to the perfection she achieves every single time.

"I wanted to sit in my favorite place with my favorite girl." He smiles over the candlelight.

"Your only girl," I remind him with a smirk. "You were busy while we were gone."

His secret spot near the lake has been transformed. The rocks have been draped in blankets and pillows, with two place settings waiting for us when we arrived. He lured me out here, reminding me that there was a meteor shower tonight. And watching nature's fireworks was a perfect ending to a stressful week.

"I had help."

I gaze across the flickering flames and smile, touched by the sentiment and amount of thoughtfulness he put into such an event. He moves the empty dishes off to the side and scoots across the blanket until our legs are touching.

"Mi amore," he says quietly as he grabs my hand. "I've been doing a lot of thinking."

"Okay." I swallow hard, my mouth suddenly dry because of the look on his face.

"Like the moon, you've locked me into your orbit since the moment our worlds collided."

I love when this man speaks to me as if we're in a romance series on the Science Channel.

"I can't imagine my life without you in it. In a few short months, you've changed everything I've ever known and made me want more out of life."

My heart races. This conversation is heavy, but he wouldn't... Would he?

He reaches underneath the pillow to his side, and I hold my breath. Maybe he would. Oh my God. He's going to ask. I gasp, suddenly unable to breathe as the moonlight radiates off the diamond like a star in the sky kissed by the heavens.

"Antonio." I cover my mouth with shaking hands.

"I can't wait any longer. I've never loved another person like I love you, Lauren. I've never wanted to settle down and have a family of my own until you came into my life. I don't want you to be my girlfriend anymore. I want you to be my wife and the mother of my children."

I hold my breath as he pauses, and tears begin to fill my eyes. When he hinted around about our future on the island, I shut him down quickly. But as each day passed, I couldn't imagine being alone again.

I wanted it all. I wanted him. I wanted the picket fence and the tiny feet running around the house with unusually loud laughter compared to their size. I wanted the American dream and everything I didn't have as a child.

"Yes!" I screech and fling myself into his arms, peppering his face with kisses. "Yes."

He laughs and pulls away, still holding the ring in his hands. "I didn't ask yet."

"Get to it, Forte. Stop beating around the bush." I wiggle my fingers near the ring, unable to wait any longer.

My entire body is shaking. I don't remember the last time I was this excited. It was probably something work-related, but for the life of me, I can't remember. But this day, this moment, I'll remember forever. Sitting in Antonio's private spot as the Perseid Meteor Shower plays over our heads.

Antonio leans forward, bending down on one knee. "Lauren Bradley, will you do me the honor of becoming my wife?"

"Yes," I say again with just as much enthusiasm as I did a moment ago before he slips the ring on my finger. It's by far the biggest rock I've ever seen other than those in museums which show off the excesses of royals around the world. "It's so beautiful."

He falls backward and takes me with him. "I love you, Lauren. You've made me the happiest man tonight."

"I love you too, Antonio."

But I know there is one more thing I have to do, and Antonio isn't going to like it. It needs to be done. I have to be free.

Antonio

I was practically buzzing by the time we walked back to the house just after the moon rose high enough to block out the meteors. Lauren said yes, and soon she'd be my wife. Sleep was impossible; my system was too hyped to get any rest.

I stared at her for hours, watching her sleep so soundly with a hint of a smile on her face. Soon she'd be Mrs. Forte, and I'd do everything in my power to make her happy.

"Couldn't sleep?" Mamma asks as she enters the kitchen just after six.

"I tried."

She grabs a mug from the cabinet and pours herself a cup of coffee before joining me at the table. "It didn't go as you hoped?"

"She said yes, Mamma."

My mother's face lights up at the news. "You've made me a happy woman this morning, Antonio."

"I've never been happier in my life."

The words I speak are the truth. Never have I experienced the euphoria I do in Lauren's presence. Everything, even down to the most mundane chore, is thrilling and somehow interesting when I have her to share it with.

"Why couldn't you sleep?"

"I'm worried I'm going to mess it up," I admit, turning the coffee mug in my hands.

"Marriage isn't easy. You'll make mistakes like every person does when finding their way on a new path. My mother gave me the best advice just after I married your father." She glances out the window, staring off into the distance. "She said to never go to bed angry. That was her key to a happy and long marriage."

"That's it?"

"When that doesn't work, she said to drink plenty of wine."

I laugh and remember my grandmother. The portly woman who wore nothing but black for the last twenty years of her life because her husband had died.

"It always helped me with your father, especially once you kids were born." She laughs as she lifts the mug to her lips. "I miss him so much, Antonio."

"I know, Mamma. He'll be home soon."

"I know. I wouldn't trade a day of my heartache because I married the love of my life."

I understand her words. There have been days I've felt anguish with Lauren, like when Trent snatched her away. But even during those times, I never once wished I hadn't met her. I live with no regrets, especially when it comes to her.

"Don't bury yourself in work either. Life is too short to be stuck in an office."

"Tell that to Lauren," I sigh. "I fear she'll work herself into an early grave."

"Find a way to change her mind."

"How?"

"A baby often puts life into perspective."

"Mamma." I shake my head and close my eyes. "I can't force her to have a child."

"Wine, my son. Wine."

Chapter 25

Antonio

"Stop touching it." Stefano smacks my hands away from my bow tie. "I can't keep fixing it."

The tiny scrap of fabric feels more like a noose than a decoration. My palms are sweaty, and I can't seem to stand still. I've never been this nervous in my life, not even when I asked Lauren to marry me.

"Don't," he says as I start to reach for it again.

"We should've gotten married on the beach in the Bahamas."

Stefano shoves a glass of whiskey in my face, urging me to drink. "Your island is too small for all of us."

I chug it down without taking a breath and hand off the empty glass to him. "Lauren never should have let Mamma plan the wedding. She turned it into the affair of the century."

"It'll be fine. By the end of today, it'll all be just a memory." Stefano smiles as he refills my glass. "One more and then I'm cutting you off. Mamma will have my balls if I let you get drunk."

There's a light knock on the door, but I let Enzo answer it because he's the closest, and I'm too busy with my second glass of whiskey.

Mamma steps inside carrying a small envelope in her hands. She kisses my brothers before she steps in front of me. "My son. You look so handsome today," she says.

I kiss her cheek, careful not to mess up her makeup. "Thanks, Mamma."

"I saw Lauren. She's stunning in her gown."

"Is she okay?"

I hated being away from her last night. Spending the night apart the evening before the wedding is a silly tradition, but one my mother had insisted that we observe. My brothers took it upon themselves to take me out for a final hurrah before my life changed forever. It was just another excuse to get drunk and party a little too hard at their age, but I indulged them. I was the only one who woke up without a headache this morning.

"She's fine, dear. She's a little nervous, but she's in better shape than I was when I married your father."

"You were nervous?"

My mother always seems so put together and in control of her emotions. She's loving but calculated in everything she does, and she has always carried herself with a certain sense of self. To think of her nervous about anything is almost absurd.

She nods as she hands me the envelope, closing my fingers around the paper. "Don't read this until I leave, and do it alone. And yes, I was nervous about our wedding night mostly."

"I don't want to know." I laugh and carefully kiss her cheek again. "Go be with Lauren. She needs you," I tell her.

Today won't be an easy day for her. As a little girl, Lauren dreamed of her wedding day. She'd told me as much. She'd thought her mother would button up her dress and give her sage advice before her father walked her down the aisle. But none of her dreams would become a reality with both of her parents gone.

"I'm going. Do not get your brother drunk," she tells Stefano.

"Mamma," he says like he's insulted.

"The priest will be in here soon to escort you to the altar."

My mother leaves without another word, and I glance down at the envelope with my name scrawled across the front. To my surprise, it isn't written in my mother's handwriting, but it's Lauren's familiar cursive style.

"Give me a minute," I say to my brothers and wave the envelope in the air. "I'd like a moment in private."

I'm certain the words inside aren't bad. My mother wouldn't deliver bad news without a warning. Or at least, I don't think she'd bring me something without knowing what it was first.

Enzo, Stefano, and Marcus leave the room and shut the door quietly behind them. I sit on the couch at the opposite end of the room, resisting the urge to pull the bow tie away from my throat.

Slowly, I tear open the envelope, carefully unfolding the delicate pieces of white paper inside. I lean back and prepare myself for anything.

My darling Antonio,

Six months ago, you walked into my life and changed everything in an instant. You were my Big Bang, causing every particle and atom in my soul to burst into life. Before you said hello, I'd been walking in darkness without any real purpose.

I tried to forget you. I tried to move on. You weren't Lou, and I wasn't Elizabeth, no matter how badly we wanted to be. But being the man you are, you didn't give up and chased me until I had no fight left in me.

As you said before, our orbits are locked together. You are my sun, the giant, shining star that chased away the darkness and cold that had filled my world.

All the things I accomplished before you hold little meaning. There's no point in victory without someone to share in the tiny moments that dot our brief lives in a seemingly endless universe.

I've put a lot of thought into our future and everything that you dream for us to be. Your dreams are mine as we're about to say I do and became a single entity, forever locked together in wedded bliss.

I want nothing more than to hear the patter of tiny feet as our children play. I want their laughter and tears and everything in between. I want to leave behind a piece of us when our time here is up. Something that only we created through the true miracle of life. Not something we built with our hands or constructed out of a pile of scrap, but a sacred moment that is truly a blessing from the heavens.

The thought of having a family had always scared me. After losing my parents and being left alone, I never wanted to face that heartache again. But I can no longer deny myself a chance at happiness. I can no longer deny you the thing you want the most. I want us.

I want our children to know their family and grow up in Italy, surrounded by nature's beauty and so much love that they'll never know the sadness I've endured.

I want the family I never had.

Because of this, effective January 1st, I'll be stepping down as CEO of Cozza Interstellar and starting on my new journey.

You've taught me that life is too short to be trapped in a boardroom. I've achieved everything I ever wanted to in business and fulfilled my father's dream. To continue my legacy, and that of our families, you better knock me up fast because it takes many years to grow a small tribe.

I'm laying down the gauntlet, Mr. Forte. Will you accept the challenge?

I've never been more excited about a journey and the unknown, but I know with you by my side, the best is yet to come.

Love Always,

Lauren xoxoxo

I stare at the piece of paper in my hand in complete shock. It takes a full minute after I read the last line before I can even muster a single word.

Every ounce of nervous energy leaves my system. No longer am I worried that she's second-guessing her decision to become my wife.

"It's time," Stefano says, opening the door slowly as I sit stunned on the couch.

"I'm ready," I tell him as I climb to my feet with my bow tie still perfectly intact.

I've never been more ready for anything in my life.

Lauren

He's there.

Standing at the altar, waiting to be mine.

"You ready, kid?" Mr. Grayson asks at my side.

When he heard about our wedding, he insisted that he walk me down the aisle. It was a little surprising, but I politely accepted his invitation. No one else had been as kind and supportive of me at Interstellar than him.

"I am," I say and take a step forward, holding on to his arm. "Thank you, Mr. Grayson."

He pats my hand and smiles. "Anything for you, my dear girl."

Antonio hasn't taken his eyes off me. The look in his eyes is similar to the first time we stood in a boardroom together. All the guests have stood and are watching as I glide down the aisle as gracefully as I can in the heels and puffy dress that I just had to have. I wanted to be the princess I'd always imagined when I was a little girl.

By now, Antonio's read the letter and knows that not only am I marrying him, I'm going all in. I no longer want to spend my life locked away in my office while the rest of the world lives. I want more than I've ever allowed myself to dream.

The trip up the aisle passes in a blur because I haven't stopped staring at the man who will be my husband long enough to focus on anyone else. He meets us at the base of the altar with his hand extended and a smile on his face.

"Mi amore," he says softly as he takes my hand in his.

"Mio marito," I whisper.

Mr. Grayson releases my hand and disappears toward the crowd that is still on its feet.

My eyes are locked with Antonio's as we ascend the steps to say our vows. I don't have a single doubt as I'm staring into the eyes of the man I love. The eyes that hold my future."

The End...

Other Books by Chelle Bliss

~MEN OF INKED SERIES~
THROTTLE ME - Book 1
HOOK ME - Book 2
RESIST ME - Book 3
UNCOVER ME - Book 4
WITHOUT ME - Book 5
HONOR ME - Book 6
WORSHIP ME – Book 7

~ALFA PI SERIES~
SINFUL INTENT- Book 1
UNLAWFUL DESIRE - Book 2
WICKED IMPULSE - Book 3

~STANDALONE BOOKS~
MISADVENTURES OF A CITY GIRL
REBOUND NOVELLA
ENSHRINE
TOP BOTTOM SWITCH
DIRTY WORK
DIRTY SECRET
UNTANGLE ME
KAYDEN THE PAST

chellebliss.com/books

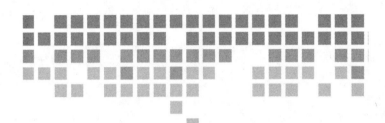

About the Author

Chelle Bliss is the USA Today bestselling author of the Men of Inked and ALFA P.I. series. She hails from the Midwest, but currently lives near the beach even though she hates sand. She's a full-time writer, time-waster extraordinaire, social media addict, coffee fiend, and ex high school history teacher. She loves spending time with her two cats, alpha boyfriend, and chatting with readers. To learn more about Chelle, please visit *chellebliss.com*.

Join Chelle's Newsletter
www.chellebliss.com/newsletter

Chelle's TEXT Alerts (US Only)
Text *BLISS* to *24587*

chellebliss.com

Enshrine

NOW AVAILABLE

Download the eBook at

chellebliss.com/enshrine

PROLOGUE

Quick.

Name the five most important things in your life. My list would've gone a little something like this: job, apartment, friends, money, and clothes.

My list was filled with frivolous things. I mean, who says shoes as one of the most important things in their life?

Me.

I glance around the bar and wonder how I got here. How did I become the girl who cares about material things and has lost sight of the important things in life? I always assumed I'd have a family by now, but you know what they say about assuming.

Becca, my best friend, snaps her fingers in my face. "Cal, are you listening to me?"

I smile and nod, but her words are distant. I've looked at my phone at least fifty times today. I'm on pins and needles waiting for an important phone call. One that could change my life, and I haven't told a soul about it—not even Becca. Telling people makes it real, and I'm not ready to face the possibility I could have more important things to deal with than which pair of shoes to wear with my favorite Donna Karan dress.

"So what do you think?" Becca asks.

I blink a few times and pretend I heard her question. "You should do it."

"Okay," she says and hops off the stool.

I grab her hand, holding her next to me so I can find out exactly what I told her to do. "Where are you going?"

"I asked if I should try to fuck 'The Butcher.'"

My mouth drops open and my eyes grow as wide as saucers. "Becca!" I yell and wrap my fingers around her hand. "Sit your ass down." I glance over my shoulder, following her eyes to where he sits.

"He's always looking over here, ogling you. I thought maybe he'd take the next best thing."

I gawk at her, completely in shock. "You can't be fucking serious."

Slowly, she walks backward toward her seat. "I'm just kidding, asshole. You acted like you were listening, but you didn't hear a damn thing. I just thought I'd fuck with you."

"I'm sorry." The guilt of ignoring her eats at me, and even though I want to tell her what's going on, I don't dare. "And for your information, Bruno isn't ogling me."

She fiddles with her cosmopolitan. "I think you should get your eyes checked next time you're at the doctor, Cal. He's always watching you. It's sexy, but it also creeps me the fuck out. He's so dangerous."

I laugh, playing it off, but I've noticed it too. "Is he looking over here now?" I ask, refusing to turn around to look for myself.

She leans forward, her eyes peering behind me. "He is. He's not taking his eyes off us either."

"He probably thinks we're trouble or something," I say and hope she drops the topic because I'd rather find out what she was going on about before.

"You can pretend like you don't think he's hot, Cal, but I've seen you flirt with him more than once."

I shake my head and chuckle softly. "Smiling and saying hello isn't necessarily flirting."

"He has a thing for you."

"He probably has a thing for every girl in this place."

"Nope." She shakes her head vigorously and puckers her lips. "He wants you."

"Enough about him." I glance over my shoulder and meet his eyes, but I quickly turn around as soon as I'm caught looking. "What did you ask before?"

"I broke up with Terrance. I want to know if you think it was a bad decision."

I never liked Terrance. From the moment I met him, he made my skin crawl. Sometimes, I'd get a feeling about a person when something wasn't right, and Terrance definitely fit the bill. "Why? What happened?" I already know the answer. He'd do weird shit all the time. Things that would never make any sense unless he was trying to hide something.

"I found messages on his phone from another woman." She frowns and brings the glass to her lips as she waits for me to answer.

"You know unfaithfulness is a deal-breaker for me too."

"Yeah." She sighs around the rim of the glass. "I hate cheating bastards. I kicked his ass to the curb." She starts to giggle.

"You okay, Bec?" I ask because she's verging on hysterical and manic.

She wipes her eyes, removing the tiny tears that have started to trickle down her cheeks. "Totally. Never been fuckin' better."

"Okay." Her behavior isn't very Becca-like, but I figure the two cosmos she's consumed have helped her feel a bit more relaxed.

"Do you think he's a cheater?" Her eyes stray from me and land on Bruno, who I assume is still seated at the bar facing us.

"Probably. He has a dick, doesn't he?" I reply and take a sip of my martini. The very thought of the man has made my body tingle for years. Maybe it's the way he looks at me or maybe it's the size of his body—he does something to me. Something no one else has ever done with a single glance.

"Yep. I mean, that man probably couldn't be faithful a day in his life."

"Probably not." I frown behind my glass.

"Like, right now, there's a girl hanging all over him. She's probably his side piece of ass."

I turn quickly, wanting to get a look at her, but he's alone when I peer over at him and not looking at me, thankfully.

"Gotcha. Pretend all you want, but you want that man something awful."

I swallow down the truth. "I do not. I was just curious what type of woman he's into."

"He's into you, my friend, and you're into him. Just promise me you won't ever date him."

"I'll never date him. I promise." I roll my eyes and scoff. "You're clearly drunk. I think it's time to pack up this party because I have to work tomorrow." I sigh, knowing I'll probably get the phone call I'm dreading too.

"We can't stay for another round? I'm hoping Mr. TDH comes over here to say hello."

"TDH?" I ask, grabbing a twenty out of my purse to close out the rest of our tab.

"Tall, dark, and handsome, Cal. Come on. Lie to me some more and tell me you don't agree." She throws her money down, hops off the chair, and heads straight for him.

I chase after her, my heels clicking on the shiny black marble below. "Becca," I beg, trying to grab her hand before she reaches him.

She ignores me, walking faster so I can't catch her. I freeze when she comes to a stop in front of him. He glances over her shoulder and meets my eyes. I can feel they've widened, and I probably look like a deer in headlights. Becca chats with him, but I'm still frozen ten feet away.

They're talking, but I can't hear what they're saying. Becca peers over her shoulder and smiles before turning around. He looks at me, his eyes roaming over my body before he looks at her again. I want to disappear out of sheer embarrassment. Before I'm able to regain my senses, Becca walks away from him and beckons for me to follow.

I find my feet, walking quickly past Bruno while keeping my eyes on the floor. Even though I'm not looking at him, I can feel his eyes on me. I weave my way through the crowd and out of his line of sight. "I'm going to kill you," I say when I catch up with her.

"Why?" She smiles and grabs my hand, pulling me toward the doorway.

"What the fuck did you say to him?" I pull my arm from her grasp and keep walking.

"I told him that he should ask you out." She laughs behind me, and I turn on my heels to face her.

My heart is hammering in my chest, and I close my eyes. "You didn't!"

She snorts and covers her mouth with the back of her hand. "I didn't. You know you two wouldn't work. He's a scary criminal, and you're as pure as the driven snow."

I snorted. "Yeah, I'm pure. What did you really say to him, Becca?"

"I told him they should clean this place up. That you had gum on your dress because some asshole stuck it under the table."

He wasn't eyeing me with lust; he was checking my dress for evidence. "I hate you."

"I should've told him you want to fuck him, though," she says, pushing past me and heading out the front door.

I follow her out and come to a stop next to her near the valet stand. "I'd kill you."

Her eyes travel up my body and her lips twist. "You need to get laid. Although he isn't my first choice for you, he'd do in a pinch."

"I do not need to get laid." It's the last thing I need right now.

She knows I'm on edge. The worry has been eating me alive ever since I found out my blood work came back abnormal and I went in for more tests and an extremely painful bone marrow aspiration.

I don't see a need for us both to worry. I'll share the details with her when I know more.

She hands the ticket to the valet, and we stand side by side watching him jog through the parking lot. "I just wanted to see what you'd do if I talked to him, and you acted just like I figured you would."

"And that is?"

"You were a complete chickenshit. I know the man is scary as hell, but one night wouldn't kill you. You can hit it and quit it. I'm sure he does it all the time."

"Don't ever say those words again," I tell her and glance behind us to see who's around.

"Relax," she says before kissing me good-bye and heading toward her car as the valet pulls up.

As I get into a cab, I can't shake what she just said. She's never liked Bruno. We've talked about him more than once. He's too dangerous, and we both know it. Neither of us is built to deal with a man like him. But the idea of a one-night stand with him does make my heart go pitter-patter in my chest and my toes curl on their own.

Relax. If she knew what I was facing, she wouldn't be so quick to say that word. If Becca were in my shoes, she'd be freaking out and I'd have to talk her off a ledge. I kick off those shoes of mine when I walk into my apartment. As I get ready for bed, my mind is still whirling.

Hopefully, tomorrow I'll have the news I want to hear. Then I can "relax" and get back to my normal life where my biggest decision is what I'll wear every day.

Of course, I live in a shallow, vapid society where we're taught that things matter and make a person. I buy shoes as if I have more than two feet. So many it would make the average person's head spin. I don't skimp on clothes either, snapping up everything I love. I spend without thinking. Gliding through life like material shit matters.

We all have that moment in our lives. The one where we think we have it made. Every little piece has fallen into place. We have the job we always wanted, money in the bank, and are living life without a care in the world.

I'm there. I freaking made it.

When I was little, my mother always said, "Get a good job. You'll be able to take care of yourself and buy whatever you want. Don't rely on any man. Stand on your own two feet, Callie."

She'd be proud of me if she were still here. I don't answer to anyone but myself.

Years ago, when I lost her, I decided I'd follow her advice. I finished college, found the highest-paying job in my field, and lived without apology.

I'm self-made and completely independent.

No one tells me what to do.

But there's a problem with her advice. One I hadn't seen coming. I'd been going through life with blinders on until Dr. Craig mentioned the single word that strikes fear into every person on the planet.

After I'd walked out of his office, I'd had some life-changing realizations.

Things are just that—things. They don't make us who we are. They make us look better on the outside, even when we're hollow on the inside. They're an illusion—the shiny objects that distract us from the really important things.

Sometimes, inevitably, we all need someone. No matter how hard we try to be self-reliant, there are times when we need a shoulder to cry on or a pair of strong arms to hold us.

But as with most realizations in life, I didn't have mine until the darkness threatened to consume my world.

My life will change with a single word. Up may become down, left may become right, and nothing may make sense anymore.

Some will read this and say, "Ugh, Callie, get a grip and stop being a whiny bitch." My response is this: Walk a mile in someone else's shoes before rushing to judgment. It's always easy to assume without any real knowledge to back it up.

Everyone thinks they'll handle shit with grace, but in reality, our fears start to suffocate us.

I'm no different—my fears are many and real.

We're all fragile, filled with insecurities and worry, and we shouldn't be judged on how we behave in our darkest hour because it's never pretty.

We should be judged on our life as a whole—the way we love, how we treat others—and not how we act when our world is crumbling around us.

I close my eyes and think of my mother, the feel of her arms around me, comforting me as I drift to sleep.

CHAPTER ONE - THE MOMENT

Running late, I rush around my apartment like a maniac trying not to forget anything. It's inevitable, though; almost every day I forget something and end up going back inside. I learned to leave ten minutes early to give myself extra time.

My phone rings, and my latest and favorite ringtone— "Sugar" by Maroon 5—blares in the morning silence as I step outside.

Without thinking, I answer. "Hello."

"Ms. Gentile?"

I fumble with my keys, trying to hold my coffee while balancing the phone on my shoulder and locking the door. "Yes."

"This is Dr. Craig's office. He'd like to speak with you as soon as possible."

"I'm here." I jog toward my car, trying to keep on schedule. I have every traffic light timed. Any deviation and I'd hit the most horrendous rush-hour traffic downtown.

"Please hold, ma'am," the woman replies before the worst eighties pop music plays and I know I'm on hold.

Placing the call on speaker, I toss my purse onto the passenger seat. I balance my phone on my lap and start the car.

As I turn on the engine, I hear his voice. "Callie?"

"I'm here, Doc, but I'm late. What did the tests say?" I ask, trying to be nonchalant even though my insides are twisting into knots.

He's been good to me. Probably better than I deserve. He always squeezes me in when I'm sick, even if he has a backlog of patients for weeks.

"Can you come into my office?" He clears his throat and doesn't have the same jovial attitude he often does when I visit his office.

"Doc, just tell me. I can handle it." I check both directions, about ready to pull out, when he speaks the words I've been dreading.

"You have cancer."

Dead fuckin' silence.

Time stops.

I freeze.

My car rolls into the street, and there's a loud bang.

Everything goes black.

ENSHRINE IS NOW AVAILABLE
Download the eBook at
chellebliss.com/enshrine

Acknowledgements

I don't even know where to start with the acknowledgements for Merger. It truly take an entire team of people to get a book out into the world and this one is no exception.

Lisa Hollett, girl, thank you for editing this manuscript on the fly with only a couple of days to do it. You didn't curse at me once, well, not to my face at least. You are truly a blessing and I'll be forever grateful that we found each other. You may not like coffee, which is totally weird, but I can forget that tiny flaw.

There are people that come into our lives sometimes that are truly a blessing. Julie Deaton fell into my lap at the most perfect time and has helped me in more ways that she'll ever understand. Thank you so so much.

To Rosa Sharon and Fiona Wilson - thank you for being rockstars. You ladies have been on this far journey with me. Although I sometimes get squirrely, you're always there.

To my agent, Kimberly, thank you for putting up with my bitchy self. I'm not easy and I know it. Your support and enthusiasm is always appreciated.

I don't know who else to thank. I could write and entire book filled with thank yous, but it would be completely boring and no one would read it.

If I forgot someone, I'm sorry. I suck sometimes. My memory is shot. It's not old yet, not yet at least, but writing and running a business has my brain all over the place. It's hard to keep the simplest thing straight, let alone my memories.

Thank you to my readers for taking a chance on a new duet. I love Antonio and Lauren and I hope you did too!

To everyone I forgot, I'm sorry. You are just as valuable and loved. I'd be nothing without the people surrounding me.